LP HALL

Hall, Billy.
Cambden's Crossing : Billy
Hall.

D1714584

ATCHISON LIBRARY
401 KANSAS
ATCHISON, KS 66002

SPECIAL MESSAGE TO READERS

This book is published under the auspices of

THE ULVERSCROFT FOUNDATION

(registered charity No. 264873 UK)

Established in 1972 to provide funds for research, diagnosis and treatment of eye diseases. Examples of contributions made are: —

A Children's Assessment Unit at Moorfield's Hospital, London.
•
Twin operating theatres at the Western Ophthalmic Hospital, London.
•
A Chair of Ophthalmology at the Royal Australian College of Ophthalmologists.
•
The Ulverscroft Children's Eye Unit at the Great Ormond Street Hospital For Sick Children, London.

You can help further the work of the Foundation by making a donation or leaving a legacy. Every contribution, no matter how small, is received with gratitude. Please write for details to:

**THE ULVERSCROFT FOUNDATION,
The Green, Bradgate Road, Anstey,
Leicester LE7 7FU, England.
Telephone: (0116) 236 4325
In Australia write to:
THE ULVERSCROFT FOUNDATION,
c/o The Royal Australian College of
Ophthalmologists,
27, Commonwealth Street, Sydney,
N.S.W. 2010.**

CAMBDEN'S CROSSING

Wyoming Territory had granted the vote to women and they could now hold elective office. For Pinkerton range detective Levi Hill, the assignment was simple: protect the life of a woman whilst she was running for justice of the peace and town marshal. But the depth of opposition to the woman was so great that Levi's life was constantly on the line. The question was: would he be man enough to fight his way out of trouble?

Books by Billy Hall
in the Linford Western Library:

KID HAILER
CLEAR CREEK JUSTICE
THE TEN SLEEP MURDERS
KING CANYON HIDEOUT
MONTANA RESCUE

BILLY HALL

CAMBDEN'S CROSSING

Complete and Unabridged

LINFORD
Leicester

LP
WEST   7 - 2000

First   by
    Hall, Billy.
    Cambden's Crossing / Billy

First Linford Edition
published 2000
by arrangement with
Robert Hale Limited
London

The moral right of the author
has been asserted

Copyright © 1999 by Billy Hall
All rights reserved

British Library CIP Data

Hall, Billy
    Cambden's Crossing.—Large print ed.—
    Linford western library
    1. Western stories
    2. Large type books
    I. Title
    823.9'14 [F]

    ISBN 0–7089–5707–2

Published by
F. A. Thorpe (Publishing)
Anstey, Leicestershire

Set by Words & Graphics Ltd.
Anstey, Leicestershire
Printed and bound in Great Britain by
T. J. International Ltd., Padstow, Cornwall

This book is printed on acid-free paper

1

It was the faintest of noises. A boot crunched on dry grass. It barely whispered through the sleep that shrouded his brain. Even so, it set off alarms in the wakeful center of his mind. He didn't even have time to react to it.

A brusque voice, vibrant with wrath, yelled, 'You! Outa that bedroll an' on your feet! Now!'

Levi silently cursed himself. His heart pounded. His muscles tensed. He opened his eyes slightly, willing himself to remain still. He feigned lingering sleepiness to frantically assess any chance of resistance.

The strident voice screamed again. 'I said, 'Now!' If you ain't out'n that bedroll in three seconds you're gettin' both barrels right in the middle. Now move!'

The experience was as new as it was unwelcome. Never, in all his years as a range detective, had anyone succeeded in slipping up on Levi Hill without waking him. Now he eyed the woman on the other end of the double-barrelled shotgun warily.

The twin barrels of that shotgun looked big enough to crawl up into. Sickening tightness gripped his gut. He forced his voice to be slow and calm. 'I ain't got my boots on.'

The twin barrels did not waver. 'I don't care if you ain't got no pants on! I said outa that bed! I don't care if'n you ain't wearin' nothin' or what's hangin' out or not hangin' out. Just git outa there! An' keep your hands right out here where I can watch 'em.'

Levi eased slowly from his bedroll as he sized up the inexplicably furious woman. She stood nearly as tall as his own five seven. Her shoulders were at least as broad as his own. Chestnut hair, streaked with gray, billowed from beneath the beat-up hat. The wide brim sagged around a face whose jowls sagged just as badly. Her feet, clad in a man's work-boots, were spread wide and planted solidly on the ground. The hands that held the shotgun unflinchingly pointed at his belly button were gnarled and calloused by hard work.

'One tough woman,' Levi told himself silently. He stood slowly, reluctantly. He felt as if he were committing suicide. Every inch he moved, moved him further from the forty-five beneath the rolled-up coat he had been using as a pillow. Not to move in the face of those twin muzzles, was just as suicidal. Aloud he said. 'I don't know who you think I am, but I'm not here looking for trouble.'

'Well you found it anyway,' she asserted. 'Anyone that comes trespassin' on my land, lettin' his horse eat my grass, an' thinkin' he can just crawl into the nest wherever he wants to without even askin', is lookin' fer trouble. Now start walkin'.'

Levi held his hands, palms toward the woman, well away from his body. 'Where am I walkin' to?'

'Where I tell ya to walk, that's where. Right straight across the crick and up that hill to the edge of my land. An' don't try nothin', or I'll blast you right in the middle.'

Levi continued to force his voice to be calm, reasonable. He took on a deliberately conciliating tone. 'Well, now, I'm perfectly willing to get off your land, and apologize for being on it in the first place, because I certainly wasn't trespassing deliberately. If you want me off your place, though, I do need to have a chance to roll up my bedroll and collect my horse.'

'You don't need nothin'!' she yelled again. 'I'll toss your stuff off'n my property sooner or later, an' you can gather it then. I ain't gonna have you jerkin' no hide-out gun outa somewheres and tryin' to shoot me, so you ain't touchin' nothin'. Now march!'

Walking stocking-footed was little different from walking in moccasins, so it didn't bother Levi nearly as much as he pretended. He was every bit as much at home in the soft-soled footwear of the Shoshone Indians as he was in riding boots. He appeared, however, as awkward and uncomfortable as possible. He limped and hobbled along, flinching and cringing from every rock and stick he felt beneath his feet. He was rewarded by her derisive snort at every flinch and groan.

The woman followed, close on his heels. As they passed through a clump of willows and brush, Levi continued his pretense of being barely able to walk. He thought he heard her almost chuckle once as he yelped at the pretended pain of stepping on a sharp rock.

As he hobbled along he slowed enough so that the barrel of the shotgun was almost against his back. He moved a larger branch out of his way, holding it carefully as he moved past it. When he released it, it snapped back, catching the woman across the side of the face.

The unexpected blow from the branch diverted her attention for the barest instant. It was all Levi needed. Moving with the speed and grace of a mountain lion, he whirled. He shoved the barrel of the shotgun skyward. One barrel discharged into the air. The kick of the gun firing helped to dislodge it. Levi jerked it, wrenching it swiftly from her surprisingly strong grip. In a continuing motion, he swept his foot behind hers, kicking her feet forward, landing her flat on her back in the brush.

His motion continued as he spun in a complete circle, bringing him back to face her. The shotgun was now in his hands, just as steadily pointed at her as it had been at him.

'Why, you . . . ' she spluttered. She swore roundly. 'You just wait till I get my hands on you, you . . . '

'You already had your chance,' Levi

said evenly. 'Now the shoe's on the other foot, and the gun's in the other hand. Get up. Let's walk back to my bedroll. I still want to put my boots on.'

She glared daggers at him for a long moment, then heaved herself to her feet. Keeping enough distance to prevent her trying his own ruse on him, Levi followed her back to where he had slept.

He was still silently cursing his own carelessness. He always selected a campsite where nobody could slip up on him unheard. He always slept as lightly as a cat. He never allowed himself to be in a position like he had found himself this morning. It was a life and death matter. Today his one lapse had nearly made it a death matter.

He had just camped too hurriedly last night. He had expected no trouble. Not yet, certainly. He had ridden until well after dark, using the moonlight as long as possible. He had too much ground to cover, and not enough time to cover it. Even as he mulled over his excuses for camping so carelessly last night, he knew there was not an acceptable excuse among them. He had just allowed himself to get careless. He had been forcibly reminded of the price of carelessness. It would not happen again. Another unwelcome thought intruded itself into his musings. Maybe he was getting enough older to sleep more soundly. He instantly shoved the frightening thought from his mind.

'Sit down over there on that rock,' he ordered.

The woman glared at him in silence, slowly complying. Levi retrieved his forty-five from beneath what served as his pillow, dropping it into his holster. He picked up his boots and walked to another large rock. He sat down, placing the shotgun so it still pointed at the woman, where he could grab it before she could heave herself from the rock she sat on.

Watching her closely, he brushed the dirt and grass from his socks and pulled his boots on. When he was finished, he spoke again. 'Who are you, and why'd you think you needed to wake me up with a shotgun?'

She glared at him for another long moment before she answered. 'I woke you up with a shotgun because you're trespassin' on my property. That's all the reason I need.'

She paused a moment. She studied him from under lowered brows, then asked, 'You work for Cambden, don't you?'

'What makes you think that?'

'Why else would you be here? I've seen your kind afore. 'Specially the past few weeks.'

'It didn't cross your mind I might just be some driftin' cowpoke, lookin' for work?'

She snorted. 'Fat chance! Just driftin', just happened to nest just over the ridge from my place. You think I was born yesterday, or what? If you're just driftin', then you're driftin' towards Cambden's. Just one more gun hand on your way to work for the almighty Elijah. I thought at least I could run one of you outa the country afore you got there.

Levi felt his interest peak. 'That so? Who are you?'

She continued to glare at him. Her mouth opened several times. Each time she shut it again before she spoke. Finally she said, 'As if you didn't know! My name's Victoria Herder.'

Levi's eyebrows shot up. He looked the woman up and down again. He laughed unexpectedly. 'Is that a fact?'

The woman swore again. 'Now why's that so funny?'

Levi's laugh faded and his face sobered, but his eyes continued to dance. 'Victoria Herder, huh? Well what'd'ya know! Victoria Herder, the newly announced candidate for Washakie County Justice of the Peace, and marshal of Cambden's Crossing, if I'm not mistaken.'

A hint of caution and fear edged out the belligerent glare of the woman's anger. 'So you are here to work for Cambden,' she stated.

Levi smiled tightly. 'Nope. You can relax. I sure ain't workin' for Cambden. You ever hear of William Bright?'

Victoria snorted. 'Who hasn't? He's the political bigshot that lives down at South Pass City. He thinks he'll be the next territorial governor. Then with that under his belt, he can move Wyoming into statehood and be a national celebrity. What about him?'

'He was one of the people that managed to get women the right to vote in the territory,' Levi reminded her. 'He introduced that legislation.'

She shrugged. 'Everyone knows that. If it wasn't fer that, I wouldn't be runnin' fer JP.'

'And marshal.'

She nodded and echoed his words. 'And marshal.'

'He thinks you have a pretty good chance of being elected.'

11

She snorted. She shuffled her feet. She squared her shoulders. 'He doesn't know Cambden, huh?'

Levi grinned. 'Well, as a matter of fact, he does. That's where I come in.'

'Is that so? And just who are you?'

Levi lifted his hands and looked up at the sky. He spoke in exaggerated tones, as though pleading with the heavens. 'Well! She finally got around to asking for my name,' he said.

He lowered his hands and looked back at Victoria. A hint of a smile toyed at the corners of his mouth. 'I'm Levi Hill.'

Surprise registered in her face. 'The Pinkerton guy?'

He nodded curtly. 'The Pinkerton guy.'

'What're you doin' clear up here? An' what's it got to do with me?'

'Well, like I said, William Bright thinks you have a very good chance to be elected. He's hoping you do. He thinks it will vindicate his efforts

12

to get the legislation passed, allowing women to vote and hold elected office. Wyoming's the first in the nation to do that, you know. You're running in Washakie County. Esther Morris is running at South Pass City, down in Fremont County. He figures Morris has a pretty good chance of being elected. A lot of folks are pretty wrought up about it, but all the opposition down there is verbal. People just do a lot of talk, but the election will go on without any problem. But this part of the territory is a different story, and he knows it. Especially with Elijah Cambden as powerful as he is around here. He thinks Cambden will do whatever he needs to do, to keep you from getting elected.'

'He's right, too,' she agreed. 'There ain't no way to argue with that at all. He's already shippin' in hired guns and threatenin' people with what all's gonna happen if I get elected.'

Levi nodded. 'That's why Bright and some others hired Pinkerton to oversee the election. They want to do whatever it takes to guarantee it's a free and fair election.'

'So they hired Pinkerton? Why didn't they just send in a bunch o' US Marshals, or maybe the army?'

Levi sighed. 'Politics. Too many people in high places don't really want this to happen. A lot of people backed the legislation as a joke, because they didn't think it'd pass anyway. Then, when it did, it wasn't such a good joke. Now they're raisin' all the objections they can, so the army wouldn't be that good an idea. They'd have to do it, if they were ordered to, but they'd be slow enough to make it look like they tried, but just got there too late. The army especially has never been real excited about seeing women get to do anything they haven't always done. No, they decided if it's going to be a fair election, it'll have to be done by someone above the control of politics. So they hired Pinkerton.'

'And, as pertneart everyone in

14

Wyoming Territory knows, you work for Pinkerton.'

'And I work for Pinkerton. They sent me to be sure nothing happens to you between now and the election, and to be sure the election's fair.'

'All by yourself? I heard stories about how you're a one-man army, but I ain't never believed it.'

Levi shrugged. 'Me neither. But I don't need to be. I can call on whatever help I need. If I need help, I can wire the governor or Bright, either one, and they'll send as many other Pinkertons, or US Marshals, or whatever I ask for. Pinkerton's has a small army of their own if they want to use it. I never have, and I don't want to. Too many of their men are just outlaws at heart. They're too hard to control. I figure I can get it done by myself.'

She digested the information slowly. Finally she stood up. The belligerence returned to her stance. Her chin lifted. 'Well, you can just turn around and go right there, and tell Mr

William Bright and all his blubber-gut politicians, with their fancy starched ruffled shirts an' stand-up collars, an' lily white hands with their nice clean fingernails, that Victoria Herder don't need no Pinkerton man nursemaidin' her. If'n I can't take care o' myself afore the election, I sure can't take care o' the county afterwards. 'Sides, I ain't gonna be beholden to none o' them pasty-faced, jack-in-the-box politicians fer nothin'. Now get your horse and roll up your bed and gimme back my shotgun and get off my property!'

Levi smiled tightly as he considered her words. He stood up. 'Naw, I guess I can't do that. I've never walked away from a job yet without giving it my best shot. I don't guess I will this one either. You don't have to like it. I'll just see what I can do to at least keep you from getting shot in the back, and make sure the election gets held on time, with no problems.'

Anger flashed in her eyes again. She held her tongue as she thought about it. The fire slowly died out in her eyes. She chewed her lower lip. Finally she shrugged her shoulders. Her answer was his biggest surprise in a morning that had already held far more than its quota of surprises. 'Well, I guess I can't run you outa the county. I tried. You do what you gotta do.' Then she waggled a finger at him. 'But don't expect me to hide behind you or your reputation, or come crawlin' to you if'n somethin' ain't workin' out right. I don't need no man to take care o' me.'

Must be a lot more scared than she's willing to admit, Levi told himself silently. I thought that'd be a regular cat-fight to get her to agree to even let me stay in the country.

Aloud, he said, 'Fair enough.' He changed the subject quickly. 'Did you say Cambden's already been hiring gun hands?'

She nodded. 'A couple or three, anyway. Just that I know about fer sure. Not that he needs 'em. The whole county's beholden to 'im, one way or another. He owns most o' Cambden Crossin' outright. It ain't likely that anyone's gonna buck 'im hard enough to elect a woman.'

Levi thought about it. 'Well, you never know. That's the beauty of a secret ballot. He can't retaliate against the ones that vote the wrong way, if he doesn't know who voted how. At least folks ought to have a fair chance. You live close to here, did you say?'

She hesitated only an instant, then waved a hand toward the east. 'Just over the ridge.'

Levi's eyes twinkled suddenly. 'Then I'll tell you what you could do. You could just invite me over to your house for some coffee and a bite of breakfast, and we'll talk about it. Somebody went and rousted me outa bed before I even had a chance to make any coffee.'

It was her turn to consider it. Her answer surprised him yet again. 'Well, you're already on my place. I guess I either gotta run you off or invite you

18

in fer breakfast. Since you ain't gimme back my shotgun yet, I can't run you off. Git your stuff picked up an' catch up yer horse. I'll throw some spuds in the skillet.'

She turned and began to walk away. Levi called her. 'Hey. You forgot your shotgun. Wouldn't want you to run into a bear on the way home.'

He carefully lowered the hammers on the shotgun, then tossed it to her. She caught it deftly and whirled, walking away with long strides.

Levi watched her go. 'Not that you'd need it, just for a bear,' he mumbled. 'All you'd need for a bear is a willow switch. And I'm supposed to protect you?'

2

The ranch house was as neat and clean as Levi had anticipated it would be. The main room held a cook stove with an oven and a warming oven. The stove top boasted four round lids, and one long lid that ran the full length of one end of the stove. They each had a notch for the handle to fit into, so they could be removed to add wood or coal. A shelf above the stove, attached to the stove back, held an enameled roaster with a rounded content covered with a dish towel.

She's got a batch of bread raisin' already, Levi commented silently. That means she was already up and made bread before daylight, because she spotted my camp over the ridge right at daylight.

'You got a pretty early start on the day,' he said.

She looked sharply at him. 'How'd you know that?'

He nodded toward the bread dough on the shelf above the stove. 'Your bread's about raised already.'

She glanced at it, then back at him. 'Is that what makes you a detective? Seeing stuff like that?'

He shrugged. 'Keeps me alive, sometimes. You have a nice house here.'

'Thanks. Hank built it. I helped 'im, o' course. He wanted me to have a pretty place to live.'

The idea that she had been married was a new thought to Levi. Somehow he couldn't imagine this hardened, muscular, square-jawed, hulking mass of self-sufficiency being somebody's wife. But he couldn't miss the note of tenderness in her voice when she mentioned him. 'What happened to your husband?' he asked.

For the barest instant tears threatened to soften the hard eyes, but they were blinked back at once. She quickly turned her back to him, fussing with the food cooking on the stove. She spoke over her shoulder. 'Horse throwed him. Busted his neck.'

'I'm sorry.'

She shrugged. 'It don't hurt so much no more. We'd already proved up on both places. I filed homestead on one spot, and him on the spot next, you see. Then we bought out a couple more places folks had proved up on. That was afore Cambden started runnin' anyone outa the country that tried to file on anything with water. We was sorta hopin' to maybe have some kids too, but . . . ' Her voice trailed off into nothing.

'I'm sorry,' Levi said again. He could think of nothing else to say.

An awkward silence wrapped its shroud around them as she busied herself at the stove. In a few minutes she set a skillet filled with fried potatoes mixed with some kind of meat on the table. Another skillet held two large flat pieces of the bread dough she had torn off and flattened, then fried in what smelled like bacon grease. She set it beside the other skillet on the table.

Without a word they both began to eat, washing down the food with great gulps of strong, hot coffee.

The silence had become oppressive by the time the food was gone. Levi stared into his cup. Suddenly he looked up at Victoria and said, 'Tell me something. If I'd have just told you to get lost, when you woke me up, would you have shot me?'

She stared hard into his eyes for several heartbeats, then turned her attention to her coffee. Over the rim of her cup she said, 'Not likely. But I wasn't about to let you know that.'

'What if I'd gone for my gun?'

'Then I'd have shot you.'

'Have you ever shot a man?'

'No. Never had to.'

'Could you? Kill a man, I mean.'

'I don't see why not. I've shot deer and elk and bear. I've shot rattlesnakes and 'coons an' 'most ever'thing else I've needed to. Bullets kill a man just as easy as they do an animal. They don't know the difference.'

Levi studied her face. He sipped his coffee. 'It ain't that easy, you know. Not when it gets right down to it.'

She shrugged her shoulders. 'What difference does it make? You didn't make me find out.'

Levi's eyes bored into those of the woman. 'But you're not just running for Justice of the Peace. You're running for marshal as well. If you get elected, sooner or later, someone will make you find out whether you can carry through and shoot someone if you have to. Sooner or later you'll be in a spot where you'll either kill someone or get yourself killed. Or maybe get somebody else killed that's depending on you.'

Her eyes betrayed the uncertainty she had worked so hard to conceal. She masked it as best as she could. 'If it comes to that, I'll find out. Did you know whether you could kill a man, before you did the first time?'

'No.'

'But you did.'

He nodded and sipped his coffee. He set the cup down. 'I did. But it's the hardest thing in the world to do. I was raised to believe a human life is the most sacred thing in the world. I still believe it. I won't kill a man if I have a choice. Not ever.'

'But you've killed men.'

'I've killed a lot of men. In fact, I guess I'd hate to think there's someone out there that's killed more men than I have.'

'Why?'

'Why what?'

'Why would you hate to think that? Do you want to be champion killer or something? Are you that proud of your reputation?'

He shook his head. 'No, no. Nothing like that.'

His voice took on an unaccustomed softness. 'Lord knows, nothing like that. No, I'd just hate to think there's someone out there that has a bigger load to carry than I do. You see what most people don't realize, is every man you kill stays with you for the rest of your life. You can never get away from him. And when there's been as many as there has — and mind you, I've never killed a man I didn't have to — but when there's been as many as there has, they sort of mount up into a heavy sort of cloud that rides on a man day and night. Sometimes I can feel the weight of that cloud, like the combined weight of all those men, sitting right on my shoulders. There are times when that load gets awful hard to carry.'

'Do you remember them?'

He hesitated a long moment, staring into space. When he spoke, his voice was still soft, but even more distant. 'I remember every one of them.'

'Do you remember how they died?'

He nodded slowly, somberly. 'Sure I do. I can't forget. I couldn't forget if I had to. I can close my eyes whenever I think about it, and watch every one of them die. I can see, like it's happening real slow, as the bullet rips through them. I can see, sometimes, the pieces of bone and skin and blood fly out with the bullet when it goes out the other side, and splatters on the wall or the floor or the ground or a tree. I shot a man in the face once, and I saw his teeth, three of them, come out the other side of his head. It surprised me that I could see them, and I could count them. All three pearly white teeth flying out in the middle of all that blood and stuff, and I could see them. I could count them.'

Surprise tinged her voice. 'It bothers you a lot, don't it?'

He nodded. His eyes remained distant. 'It always bothers. Especially, sometimes, at night, alone, when I'm camped somewhere. I'll hear a sound in the night and it'll sound like the step of one of the men I've killed. I'll hear a little whisper of the wind in the pine trees, and it'll sound like the breath that rattled in the throat of one of those men, as he was dying. I'll hear an eagle scream, and it'll be the voice of a man screaming in pain and fear, 'cause I shot 'im, and he knows he's about to meet his Maker. Yeah, it bothers.'

'But you'll kill again. Even knowing that it'll bother, and it'll haunt you for the rest of your life, you'll kill again.'

Levi sighed again, heavily. 'Without an instant's hesitation,' he admitted. 'If I ever let it bother me enough that I hesitate, I'm a dead man.'

'That'll happen some day,' she prophesied.

He nodded thoughtfully. 'Probably. It almost did, once. A kid came up behind me, one time. He was practising sneaking up like an Indian, he said. He was getting pretty good at it. I didn't hear him until he was almost there, and he stepped on a dry leaf. I turned around and drew. You've got to understand, I've trained myself to never draw my gun without shooting. It's got to be done all in the same motion as I draw. That's the difference, usually, between living and dying. When two men draw, the man that draws, then decides whether to shoot, dies while he's making the decision. It's got to be done without any hesitation at all, all as one motion. Well, I turned and drew my gun, and realized it was just a kid before I squeezed the trigger. I don't know how I did it. I've always thought the Lord had a hand in it. He didn't want that kid killed, or He didn't want me havin' to live with killin' a kid. Anyway, I didn't shoot. It wasn't a week later I had to draw against a real Indian. One of the Nez Percé that broke off on his own. He was sneakin' up behind me, almost the same way. I heard him, like it was just the same thing again. And I almost hesitated. If I had, I'd have been dead. The Indian lunged with his knife just as I turned, and I shot him. He cut my arm, as it was. If I'd hesitated, he'd have cut my throat. Some day it'll probably happen that way. I'll hesitate, and the other man won't.'

As though embarrassed by the uncharacteristically long monologue, Levi lapsed into silence. She did not interrupt, lost in her own efforts to fathom her resolve to kill if necessary. Suddenly, Levi's head snapped up.

'Listen!' he ordered.

'What is it?' she asked.

'Shush,' Levi whispered.

He sat there, hand suspended in air, listening. Victoria frowned, but she whispered as she asked, 'What?'

Levi frowned. 'Camp robber jay, or maybe a blue jay squawked a minute ago. Sounded like he was on that rise just south of the house.'

Victoria frowned. 'What? A bird?'

Without answering, Levi slid from his chair. He picked up his rifle where he had leaned it just inside the front door. Victoria started as he did, realizing for the first time he had brought his rifle into the house with him, and she hadn't even noticed.

Levi lifted the latch on the door quietly, then lowered it silently back into place. He stood there with his hand on the latch, frowning thoughtfully. He turned and looked at Victoria. 'Best get down on the floor,' he said softly.

Frowning her obvious confusion, Victoria slid out of her chair onto the floor. Levi squatted down low beside the door. He lifted the latch noisily and swung the door wide. Wood chips flew instantly from the edge of the door jamb above Levi's head.

Levi lunged out the door and rolled. As he came to his feet, his rifle was against his shoulder. He fired three times swiftly in the direction of the low rise, then lunged back through the door again.

He came to his feet and stood against the wall, just beside the door. There was no sound for a moment. Then brush snapped and crackled faintly from outside. Sounds of a running horse carried briefly on the breeze.

Levi lunged back through the door. He whistled sharply, 'Here, Blue!' he yelled.

The words had scarcely left his mouth when his horse galloped around the corner of the house. Levi lunged into the saddle, the rifle still in his hand. 'Catch 'im boy!' he yelled.

The horse hurtled forward, muscles bunching and stretching, accelerating until the ground was a blur beneath his feet. Levi bent low over the saddle horn, making himself as small a target as possible in case the running hoofbeats were a trick. As they topped the rise, his trained eyes instantly picked up the faint trail the running horse had left in the dew-moistened grass. Blue saw the tracks as well, following them as though in perfect harmony with his master's wishes.

The trail they followed at a dead run led across a narrow strip of grass, through a patch of marshy ground along the bottom of a swale, then across a broad meadow. At the other side of the meadow a line of dense trees and brush obscured the sight of whatever lay beyond. Levi hauled on the reins, pulling the horse to a skidding stop.

He surveyed the edge of the forest nervously. He shook his head. 'If he's layin' up in there waitin' for us, we wouldn't have a chance,' he muttered. 'If we ride all the way around, so he can't lay for us, he'll be long gone before we get there. I could track him, but I don't know if it's the thing to do, right now. He could lead us far enough away, then circle back to have another try at Victoria. Let's just let him well enough alone. I'll remember his tracks, though. We'll meet again.'

He turned his horse and trotted back to the house. He swung down, not bothering to tie the horse. He knew the well-trained animal would stay within easy calling distance of the house.

'He's gone,' he said, as he walked back inside. 'I left my horse out of sight, in the trees behind the house, so he didn't know anyone but you was here.'

Victoria was just now pulling herself

up from the floor. Her face was pasty white. Her eyes were oversize whiter circles in the white of her face. 'I knew they'd try that,' she said.

She sat down heavily on a chair. She stared at nothing for a long moment. As she turned her face toward Levi, her eyes came back into focus. The ashen pallor of her face gave way to pink, then red. Anger replaced the fear in her eyes. She swore. 'I knew they'd try that,' she repeated. 'Knew it as well's I know my name. That's why I been out 'n about ever' mornin' afore daylight, seein' who's waitin' in the bushes. That's why I was so all-fired mad when I seen you campin' there. I figgered you was one o' Cambden's gunmen, just waitin' till daylight to have a go at me.'

'They've tried this before?' Levi asked.

She shook her head. 'Not shootin' at me that-away,' she admitted. 'But three or four times they come ridin' hell-fer-leather through the yard throwin' rocks through my windows an' yellin' like wild Indians. They stuck a note to my front door with a knife tellin' me not to run fer no man's office. Stuff like that. I figgered it was just a matter o' time till they either tried to scare me good or kill me.'

Levi looked at her for a long moment. 'Did it work?' he asked softly.

'Did what work?'

'Scaring you. Are you still going to run?'

She swore a string of invectives that threatened to blister the hide off of Levi's face. When her vocabulary was exhausted, she said, 'Of course I'm still going to run. If I wasn't sure before, I am now.'

Levi nodded. 'Then I'll do everything I can do to see you get a fair election,' he said.

He wasn't sure how he was going to accomplish that. He certainly didn't know all that it was going to involve.

3

His skin tingled. A cold wind stirred the hair on the back of his neck. He resisted the urge to shudder.

The mountain meadow spread out before Levi in a profusion of wildflowers. Ringed with snow-capped mountain peaks, a small lake mirrored their rugged majesty. Soft white clouds floated in an impossibly blue sky. Tall pine and spruce drew the boundaries of the meadow, then stood in closed ranks to the edges of his vision. It was a scene of unrivaled beauty.

From the time he had left Victoria's ranch house, Levi had ridden warily. He knew trouble would come. He was braced for some sound, some slight movement, that would betray an ambush. He was almost certain one would be set for him. Now he saw the trouble, and it came in much different form than he had been expecting.

A group of men clustered half-way across the meadow. Their presence and deployment jangled alarms wildly in Levi's mind. Two men sat their saddles, obviously waiting his approach. Four others, two to each side, fanned out toward him. They were positioned so they could close in behind him as he approached the waiting pair.

'Welcome committee,' Levi muttered to his horse. 'Word gets around fast. Well, if they think I'm going to ride right into a setup that obvious, they must think I came over the mountain and left my brain on the other side.'

He nudged Blue to a brisk trot. When he was almost even with the nearest of the riders, who obviously intended to flank him, he turned his horse abruptly. He circled to his right, riding around the man, within about thirty feet of him.

The man swore and started to turn his horse. Levi spoke softly, so only that man would hear. 'Don't even think about it, friend. If you make any effort to get around behind me, I'll drop you outa that saddle before you can blink.'

The man froze. His hand hung suspended above his gun butt. He swallowed hard. Levi passed behind him. The second man was already moving his horse to outflank Levi as well. Levi spoke again, a little louder. 'Wrong direction, friend. You stay to my left, or I'll send you to hell on a hot lead wagon before you can get a thumb on the hammer.'

The man shot a quick look toward the man who was now almost beside Levi. His eyes darted over to the pair in the center, one of whom had to be the boss. By the time he had hesitated, Levi was past him.

Levi rode swiftly to the waiting pair, forcing them to turn their horses to face him. As he approached, he was now in a position to keep all six men in his field of vision.

As he reined up in front of the

pair, two of the men again began to move their horses to get behind him. Levi spoke to the older of the two men, facing his burning glare without flinching. 'You tell your boys to stay out there in front of me, or I'll shoot their horses out from under them in exactly two more steps.'

The man glared in silence. One of the men was now nearly out of Levi's field of vision. Wordlessly Levi whipped his rifle from its scabbard. In one fluid motion he turned sideways in the saddle and raised the rifle. It barked once. The horse of the rider on his left dropped to the ground. The rider rolled free, cursing loudly. Before any of the group could respond or realize what was happening, he had turned the other way, levered another shell into the chamber, and shot the horse from under the second rider.

He levered the rifle's action again, bringing it back to bear on the chest of the man to the left of the one in front of him.

He spoke to the man directly in front of him, rather than the one on whom the gun remained trained.

'Now you best tell your boys to shuck their guns in a hurry or your hired gunhand here's gonna be on the ground with them horses and you'll be right behind him.'

The man's face had turned crimson with fury as he watched the two horses get shot. Now the crimson deepened to a purple that Levi thought for a moment would precipitate a fit of apoplexy. Instead, in a voice with surprising strength and control, he called out to his hands: 'Shuck your guns, boys. He's callin' the shots. For now.'

An instant of disbelieving hesitation hung in suspense. Then all four of the outriders threw down their guns as though suddenly too hot to hold.

'Now yours,' Levi ordered the gunman.

The gunman stared back with a blank icy glare. Slowly he complied.

'Now you back your horse up about

six steps, and have them other boys move back over there where I can watch you all a little easier,' Levi ordered. 'And keep both hands on top of your saddle horn. Left hand on top of the right one. If I see your hands even twitch, I'll shoot you out of the saddle.'

The gunman glanced at the obvious boss. He nodded curtly. The gunman began to back his horse. When he was a couple lengths of the horse behind his boss he motioned the other men to join him. The two that were now afoot began walking first. They were quickly followed by the two who remained mounted. Nobody spoke until all five were grouped together. Levi had the fleeting impression one of the riders was almost smiling. He was the only one. The rest glared in unrestrained hostility.

'You owe me for two fine horses,' the man facing Levi gritted. 'I've spent twenty years buildin' up the best remuda in Wyoming Territory.

Them two horses you just shot are worth more than you can make in a year.'

Levi shook his head. 'You had your chance. I let you know twice I wasn't dumb enough to let your bully boys get around me. I told you exactly what I was going to do. If you weren't smart enough to know I'd do it, you'll just have to chalk two horses up to being the price of you being too dumb to keep 'em.'

The man's face reddened again. He slowly won the battle with his temper, and spoke. 'Just who do you think you are?'

Levi shook his head. 'Wrong question first. I'm the one calling the shots. Who are you, and why are you so anxious to put me in the middle of your boys?'

The man's eyes bored holes through Levi for a long moment before he spoke. 'My name's Cambden. Elijah Cambden. I own most of this valley. You're on my property.'

Levi shook his head. 'No I'm not.

Not here. You run cows on it, but it's government range. Your land don't start for almost seven miles. I looked up a map at the surveyor's office before I came.'

'I've run my cows on this land for twenty years.'

'I 'spect that's true enough, but that doesn't make it yours. It still belongs to the government. One of these days the government'll probably charge you to run your cows here. Either that, or they'll sell the land to someone else.'

Fire flashed from the pale blue eyes of the rancher. 'Not while I'm alive, they won't.'

'If you keep trying to box me into a corner, that may not be long,' Levi retorted. 'What's your interest in me?'

'You been over at the Herder woman's place.'

'That's a fact. I have. Is that against your rules?'

'It is if you think you're gonna help her with that crazy wild-eyed scheme o' hers. Who are you?'

Several answers ran through Levi's mind. Finally he decided to try to lower the level of the antagonism if possible. He lowered the rifle. He hooked his thumb on the hammer, squeezed the trigger, and lowered the hammer carefully. Then he dropped the rifle into the saddle scabbard. He kept his right hand inches from his forty-five. 'My name's Levi Hill.'

The name slapped against the five huddled hands with a visible jolt. Surprise flickered momentarily in the rancher's eyes as well. 'The Pinkerton guy?'

'The same.'

'What are you doin' up here?'

Levi let the question hang a long moment. Then he said, 'Pinkerton's been hired to ride herd on the election at Cambden's Crossing. Some people want to be sure it's a free and fair election, and that all the women are allowed to vote that want to vote. I'm sure you know the territorial legislature passed a law last year giving women the vote and the right to hold office.'

The rancher spat. He wiped his mouth with the back of his hand. His flashing eyes never left Levi's face. 'I'm aware of it,' he gritted, 'but it ain't gonna happen. Not in Cambden's Crossing, it ain't gonna happen. There ain't no woman ever voted in this country, and there ain't no woman ever gonna hold office in this country. Not unless they send the army, they're gonna have a bigger war'n the Nez Percés put on around here.'

Levi pursed his lips thoughtfully. He purposely kept his voice calm, reasonable, soothing. 'Well, I can understand you not liking that kind of change. It's a new way of thinking about things. But the law's the law. A man can change the law by convincing the government to change it. He can change the law by convincing all the people it's a bad law, and getting them to work on the government. But you can't change the law by fighting it. Not any more. You could do that when you staked your claim to this land twenty years ago, but that day's gone for good. All you can do that way nowadays is get yourself hurt.'

'Then I'll get myself hurt,' Cambden said flatly. 'And a lot of other people in the process. Including you, if you try to make it happen. That election'll happen all right. I guess I'm even in favor of that. We've got to have elections in a free country, but there ain't no women gonna vote in Cambden. And there sure ain't gonna be no woman elected.'

Levi's eyes went flat and hard. His voice remained soft, but its edges took on the brittle hardness of flint. 'If you want to stop it, you can try right now. I'm here to see the election happens, the sixth, right on schedule, and that no woman is denied the right to vote. If you want to stop it, you'll have to stop me. Now's as good a time as any if you want to try that. You got better numbers on your side than you'll ever get again.'

Cambden flushed red again, but he

refused the bait. 'I'll decide when it's time. There ain't no way you can protect that woman from my outfit, or any of the other outfits around here that ain't gonna let it happen. Good Lord, man, think! Do you realize what'll happen to this country if we let women vote? Or hold office? Every whore in the country will have as much right to vote as you and I do! Do you mean to tell me you want some woman like that Herder woman struttin' around wearin' a badge, tellin' you to go home now, it's too late for you to be in the saloon? Are you ready to run around sayin', 'Yes, Ma'am,' 'No, Ma'am,' 'Excuse me, Mrs Justice o' the Peace, Ma'am,' an' lettin' her tell you what you can do an' what you can't do?'

Levi sighed heavily. 'Nope, I ain't. I can't think of anything I like less than the idea of havin' a woman marshal, or Justice of the Peace. Well, to be honest, the idea of a woman Justice of the Peace ain't near as bad as the idea of a woman marshal. I got no problem with women votin' at all. That's a matter of being intelligent enough to make good choices, and I'll have to admit most of the women I've known are smarter'n most men. But there's things it just ain't proper for a woman to do, in my mind. But that's beside the point. The law's the law. If we ain't gonna follow the law, we're no better than savages. If we're going to be civilized and follow the law, we have to obey the laws we hate just as much as the laws we love.'

'In a pig's ear we do,' the rancher retorted. 'I ain't obeyin' that law, and neither's anyone else in Cambden as long as I'm standin'. You hear me? Now you either get outa the country or you get set to fight my whole outfit an' every other outfit in the valley. That's how it is.'

With that he whirled his horse and jammed his spurs into the animal's sides. The horse shot forward, reaching a long lope in three strides. The gunman stepped off his horse. He carefully picked up his gun and dropped it back into his holster, watching Levi carefully. Then he climbed back on his horse and spurred after the rancher. The other two horsemen picked up their guns as well, then rode to the dead horses to retrieve the saddles and bridles belonging to the hapless cowboys now afoot. Nobody looked at Levi or spoke another word to him.

Levi sighed heavily again. He lifted the reins and turned Blue back the way he had been riding. He did not look back as he left the meadow.

4

'You like shootin' at women, do you?'

Cambden's Crossing dozed in the afternoon sun. Few people were in the street. The small man with the hard face stopped in his tracks. He turned slowly toward Levi. 'You talkin' to me?'

'I am. Do you like shooting at women, or do you just get paid to do it?'

Furtive eyes darted each direction, then back to Levi. 'What are you talkin' about?'

'I'm talking about you shooting at a woman. Victoria Herder, to be exact.'

The man's eyes narrowed. 'Who are you?'

'I'm the man that was at her place yesterday morning when you put a bullet in her front door, just when you thought she was coming outside.'

The gunman's posture tensed visibly. 'I don't know what you're talkin' about. You say somebody took a shot at the Herder woman?'

'Nope. That's not what I said at all. I said you took a shot at her.'

'What makes you think that?'

'Isn't that your horse, that you just rode over from the mercantile store?'

'Yeah. So what?'

'So I tracked you away from her house, through the swamp and across the meadow, right after you took that shot. I never forget a horse's track. It was either you, or someone ridin' your horse.'

The gunman squinted against the sun, trying to fathom Levi's intention. He took a step sideways to put the sun at a better angle. As he did, Levi took a step the same direction, keeping the sun's advantage solidly in his favor. The gunman's lips tightened as he did so. 'You musta made a mistake,' he said. 'I ain't never even been on that ridge above her house.'

51

ATCHISON LIBRARY
401 KANSAS
ATCHISON, KS 66002

'Who said the shot came from that ridge?'

The gunman's lips tightened further. 'Ain't that what you said?'

'Nope. I said some sneaking coward ain't even got the guts to stand up in front of a woman took a shot at her from hiding. I didn't say anything about the shot coming from the ridge. You just knew that by yourself. I also said you are that sneaking coward, and you are under arrest for attempted murder. Now unbuckle your gun belt and let it drop.'

The gunman cursed. His hand streaked for his gun. Faster than the eye could follow it closed on the well-worn gun butt and jerked the gun from its holster.

The end of the pistol cleared the holster and started to arc upward. It was not nearly fast enough. Even as he started his move, Levi's hand blurred and his own gun seemed to leap into his hand. A narrow column of fire spouted out of the end of

Levi's forty-five, already levelled at the gunman's chest. He grunted and took a step backward. He looked down at his chest, as though trying to fathom what had struck him. His eyes came back up to meet Levi's. The gunman's right hand stayed where it was, gripping the pistol still pointing toward the ground. He opened his mouth. His voice was surprisingly clear and calm. 'Knew that'd happen sometime,' he said. 'Jeez, you're fast.'

As he said it, his eyes began to glass over. He collapsed suddenly, as if all the bones had been abruptly removed from his body, leaving only empty flesh. He landed on his side in the street. One arm remained beneath him. His knees were doubled. He looked as though he were asleep on his side, but his wide-open eyes stared sightlessly.

A crowd gathered as if by magic on the board sidewalk, half a street away. A ripple moved through the crowd, spewing a wizened frame of a man, face almost hidden beneath the broad brim of a tall Stetson. A marshal's badge reflected sun from his vest. He limped on a bad left leg as he approached Levi. 'What's goin' on here?'

'Hello, Marshal,' Levi greeted him. 'This man put a bullet into Victoria Herder's front door jamb yesterday morning. He tried to kill her from the brush above her house. I tried to arrest him for it, and he went for his gun. I had to kill him.'

The marshal glared through squinting eyes. 'Whatd'ya mean, you tried to arrest 'im? I'm the law around here. Who are you?'

'My name's Levi Hill. Pinkerton range detective. Special commission from Territorial Governor John Campbell.'

At mention of that name, the marshal's head jerked. He glanced quickly at the assembled crowd. He chewed the ends of his drooping moustache thoughtfully. 'Hill, huh? I've heard of you. But I don't know nothin' about no special commission.

Anyway, I'm the law in this town, an' there ain't no other. I'll have to ask you to gimme your gun, an' I'll be puttin' you under arrest till I get this here sorted out.'

Levi's eyes narrowed. He made no effort to surrender his gun. 'I don't want to go against you, Marshal. But you know I can't do that. I'm acting well within my authority here. Authority from the Wyoming Territory outranks the authority of a town or a local area.'

'I don't know nothin' 'bout no authority here, 'ceptin' mine. What are you doin' in Cambden's Crossin' anyhow?'

'That's what my special commission is.' He raised his voice for the benefit of the assembled crowd. 'I'm here to insure September sixth's election is fair and free, that all women of this area are allowed to vote, and to protect the folks running for office. Especially that includes insuring the safety of Victoria Herder until after the election.'

The marshal's face blanched. 'On whose orders?'

'I already told you that. Special orders of the governor of Wyoming Territory. I have the papers in my saddle-bags. I'll be happy to show them to you.'

'Lige ain't gonna like that.'

'So he told me.'

'You already talked to Lige?'

Levi nodded. 'He and a few of his boys thought they'd scare me off yesterday,' he said. 'I shot the horses out from under a couple of them.'

A ripple of sound flowed across the growing crowd. Levi ignored it. He addressed the marshal. 'I'm only here to help you with your job, Marshal,' he said. He made a special effort to keep his voice bland and even. 'I know it's a formidable job to enforce the laws of the territory during a time of change. But as a duly sworn officer of the law, I'm sure you understand how important those laws are.'

The marshal's voice took on an

almost plaintive tone. 'They shouldn't never o' passed no law givin' women the right to vote.'

'That's not really our place to decide, I guess. We all have an opinion. The fact is, they did. Now it's the law. Since it's the law, it'll be enforced. It's our job to do that.'

The marshal shook his head. 'I don't 'spect so. Not here, no ways. Lige, he already done said it ain't gonna happen in Cambden's Crossin'.'

'Lige isn't the law here.'

'Lige owns this town.'

'Lige still isn't the law here,' Levi insisted. 'Whatever he owns or doesn't own, the people of this area are free to vote for whoever they want to vote for. Our job is to see that nobody interferes with that.'

'Your job maybe. Not mine.'

'Yours if you're the marshal.'

'Not in this town. Now gimme your gun. I gotta arrest you.'

Levi scanned the rapt faces of the crowd. Most showed excited interest.

A few showed open support for his stand. He saw no indication of any strong support at all for the marshal. He turned his attention back to the lawman. 'You're Slim Collins?'

'How'd you know that?'

'The governor told me. Said you'd worked for Cambden for years, and took orders from him. Said you might not want to enforce the law here. I told him I thought any man that was a man and wore a badge would put the law over loyalty to an old boss.'

'You thought wrong. I been workin' for Lige most o' my life. I take orders from him, badge or no badge.'

Levi sighed. 'That's too bad. In that case, I'll have to relieve you of that badge. On the authority of the governor of the territory of Wyoming, I'm ordering you to hand me your gun.'

Slim's face blanched, then reddened. His moustache bristled as he spluttered, fighting to find words to express his surprise and anger. Finally, unable to put anything else into words, he spat out a long string of obscenities. Levi's calm voice interrupted the tirade. 'Your gun, Slim. Hand it over.'

Slim stood with his hand poised above his gun butt. Again, Levi's calm voice interrupted his transparent thoughts. 'Don't even think about it, Slim. You don't have a chance. You're a cowboy, not a gunman. You just watched me outdraw and shoot one of the fastest gunmen in the country. You're not even in that class. Just give me your gun. I don't want to have to kill you.'

The red of Slim's face deepened perceptibly. He hesitated for several heartbeats. 'You can't get away with this. Lige'll take you apart.'

'He might,' Levi admitted. 'Time'll tell. I'm sure he'll try. Now hand me your gun.'

Slowly Slim lifted his gun from its holster and handed it to Levi. 'Now the badge,' Levi ordered.

Slim hesitated again, then ripped the

badge from his vest and handed it over as well.

'Now, Slim, I don't want to have to lock you up. I can, you know. I can lock you in your own jail, to keep you from interfering with the law. But I don't want to do that. If you'll give me your word you'll stay out of trouble, and you won't interfere with my doing what the governor sent me here to do, I won't need to lock you up.'

Slim stared in open disbelief. He spluttered for nearly half a minute. Finally he whirled without a word and stalked away. Levi turned to the crowd. 'In case any of you didn't hear what I said, my name is Levi Hill. I'm a special Pinkerton detective, sent here by the governor of Wyoming Territory, to insure the election week after next is free and fair. All residents of this area will be allowed to vote. That means both men and women. Any resident of the area over twenty-one years old can vote. Special ballots are being printed up, and will be delivered here before the day of the election. One of the names on that ballot will be Victoria Herder. She's running both for Justice of the Peace and town marshal. To my knowledge, it's the first time in history women have been allowed to vote, anywhere in the world. It's the first time at least in this country. It's also the first time in this country a woman has been allowed to run for an elected office. That's why it's important to the territory and to the law that nothing and nobody interferes with the election. I'll be naming someone as acting town marshal in the next day or two. In the meantime, I'll take responsibility myself. Now spread the word that the election will be held on Tuesday of next week, and nobody will be allowed to interfere with it, or to influence who can and can't vote, or who they can vote for.'

An excited buzz of conversation erupted as soon as he was finished. He turned and walked away. Nobody even noticed his departure, as the whole crowd broke into excited little groups discussing his words and the events of the day.

'Sure hope I can keep all those promises,' Levi muttered to himself.

He had more than adequate cause to worry.

5

Tension crackled in the air. Levi stood with his back to the bar. Three big men faced him in a half circle.

'That's just the way it's gotta be,' Levi said.

'Not in Cambden's Crossin',' the center of the three men replied.

'That's the way it's gotta be anywhere in Wyoming Territory,' Levi argued. 'The law's the law.'

'The law here's what Lige says it is,' another of the trio responded.

'Not as long as I'm standin',' Levi disagreed.

'That ain't long,' the first speaker replied.

As he spoke, he planted his feet and swung. His huge right fist looped toward Levi's head. Levi stepped to his left, letting the fist whistle past his face. He stepped in behind it, sending a straight right to the man's chin.

His fist landed with a shock that reverberated up his arm and into his shoulder. It sounded like an axe driven into the wood of an oak tree. The man only grunted, and took a short step backwards to maintain his balance.

The man on Levi's left sent a fist toward Levi's face. He brushed it aside with his left hand and stepped into a right aimed at the man's stomach. Flesh seemed to close around his fist for an instant as it buried itself in the man's gut. He emitted an almost silent grunt and doubled over.

Lights exploded in Levi's head as a fist smashed into the right side of his face. He countered with a looping left hook that landed somewhere on the side of somebody's head.

Another fist crashed into Levi's nose. As he responded, another clubbed into his back, low down.

He fought to get clear of the bar, where he had room to utilize his feet as well as his hands. The three closed around him, not allowing him to do so. Blows rained down on him from three sides. He planted his feet, ignoring the blows, and began a concentrated effort of returning blow for blow. He put every ounce of energy and strength he could muster into each swing. He was rewarded with feeling the devastating effect of each as it landed. Blood spattered and ran, covering the faces of all four men in a matter of seconds.

Levi lost count of the blows he delivered or received. He was only aware that no matter how many he landed, or how solidly they landed, the assailants kept coming. He felt himself driven back and to the side. His boot caught something, sending him sprawling onto the floor. The blows smashing into his body changed from that of fists to that of boots, as his attackers switched to using their feet on his prone figure.

His hand brushed his gun butt. He knew they very well might beat him to death. Even so, he could not bring himself to use his gun against men who had made no effort to use their guns against him. He tried to roll aside, hoping to find something that would provide cover enough to allow him to regain his feet. The blows continued to smash into him from all sides. The room began to spin around him. Lights exploding in his head made it impossible to make out anything clearly. The taste of his own blood filled his mouth.

'Sure and that will be enough I'm thinkin'.'

Levi was only dimly aware of the voice. Its Irish accent was not lost on him, but it made no sense. Nothing made sense. Everything was swimming in a red haze of incredible pain.

Another voice spoke. He recognized it as one of his assailants. 'Get outa the way, Mulgrew. This ain't none o' your affair.'

'Sure and I'm thinkin' it may be,' Mulgrew disagreed. His voice was light, affable. 'Most fights around here are my affair, it seems. 'Tis enough of a beatin' you've given this man, I'm thinkin'.'

'It'll be enough when we say it is,' another argued.

'Oh, sure now, Tug Wilson, and are you thinkin' you can come over me to get at him some more are you? I'm thinkin' the man has given you boys almost as good as you've given him, and it'll not take me much more to put you all on the ground.'

Levi shook his head. He fought to clear his vision. He wiped his hands across his eyes, swiping the blood and sweat from them. He struggled to his hands and knees. He could see the legs and widely planted feet of the Irishman squarely in front of him.

'Lige ain't gonna like you interferin',' the spokesman of the trio gritted through bloody teeth.

Levi almost smiled at the slur in the voice. Messed his mouth up some, at least, he thought silently.

Mulgrew spoke again. 'Now sure,

John Dally, an' I thought better o' you than comin' in here to fight some other man's fight for 'im. Why wasn't you tellin' Cambden a man fights 'is own fights in this country, 'stead o' sendin' three o' his hired men to do 'is fightin' for 'im?'

Dally ignored the question. 'This guy's here from some big money outfit that hired him to come up here and tell us how to run our own business. He's got no business bein' here. Somebody's gotta run 'im out.'

'Is that a fact now? And is that your brain grindin' away, or is that a parrot I hear, sayin' what the boss man told 'im to be thinkin'?'

Levi struggled to his feet. He used his sleeve to swipe the blood out of his eyes. He squinted to focus on the three men, standing together as their leader argued with the Irishman.

Levi looked Mulgrew over. He was a huge chunk of a man. He must have stood nearly six feet four inches tall. His shoulders were so broad they threatened to split the largest shirt the mercantile store carried. His arms looked like tree limbs, ending in massive hands that hung relaxed, slightly in front of his legs. His head was thrust forward. His high forehead sloped to heavy brows that jutted out over twinkling blue eyes. Levi couldn't decide whether he was enjoying the three men's hesitancy, or hoping they would give him an excuse to wipe up the floor with the three of them.

Dally decided to ignore Mulgrew and address himself to Levi. 'This is a warning, Hill. The next time we won't go so easy on you. Get outa Cambden's Crossin'. Keep your nose outa the election. It ain't none o' your affair.'

Levi spat a mouthful of blood into the sawdust on the floor. 'It is my business, and it'll stay my business,' he said. 'If you want me outa town, you'll have to kill me. But the next time you better come at me with your guns out and blazing. I don't aim to take another beatin' from men that are too yellow to fight me one at a time.'

Mulgrew butted in. 'An' if you boys wasn't noticin', he had the chance to fill the three of you with lead, an' he didn't do it. I seen 'im, I did, brush 'is gun an' think about it. This time he decided to take a whippin' from you, instead o' killin' you. You'd best remember that. That's why I decided I'd not be lettin' you whip up on him any longer. So you whipped him, but you can be thankin' 'im for your lives, for he just plain let you live when he didn't need to.'

The three shot quick glances at each other, then back at Levi. Levi's vision was clearing enough, so he could begin to appreciate the havoc his own fists had wrought on all three faces.

'It won't happen again,' he promised softly. 'You had your chance this time. And the answer's still no. I'll be stayin' and the election will happen on schedule, and everybody will be able to vote. Nobody will tell you boys you can't vote, and you won't tell anyone else they can't. And the next time you try to interfere with me, I'll kill you. Now get out.'

The three hesitated. Mulgrew said, 'You heard the man. Be gettin' outa here. Now.'

The three whirled and left, leaving tell-tale blood spots in the sawdust as they did.

Levi sat down abruptly at one of the round tables. One of the 'working girls' walked over to him. 'Your face is a mess,' she said. Her tone was matter-of-fact, but tinged with concern. 'You better come upstairs with me and let me clean you up a little.'

Mulgrew addressed her. 'Sure, now, Constance, are you sure you want to be doin' that? Cambden will be sure to hear of it. He'll not take it kindly.'

The girl tossed her head, sending the ringlets of flame-red hair dancing around her face. 'Let him. I've been waiting a long time for someone to stand up to him and those toughs of his. They think they own the whole country and everybody in it. But now that you mention it, you aren't exactly going to be on his Christmas list either, Griff, my boy.'

Mulgrew shrugged. 'Sure an' that's as may be.'

The girl turned back to Levi. 'My name's Connie. Come on. I've got a pitcher of water and stuff up in my room.'

Levi's hesitation was so obvious Mulgrew laughed. 'Sure, man, an' you can go with 'er. She's a nice girl, Constance is. She'll not be throwin' herself at you.'

Levi clearly didn't like the idea, but his choices were limited. He struggled to his feet. Connie grabbed him by an arm, steadying him as he struggled up the stairs. He collapsed onto the bed as soon as he was inside her room. She poured water into a basin and brought it over to the bed. 'You'll have to sit up a minute, so I can get this shirt off you,' she said.

Meekly Levi obeyed. He shoved himself to a sitting position and began to struggle with the buttons. His hands were already too stiff to manage them. 'Here,' she interrupted his efforts. 'Let me do it.'

With a practiced skill he found disconcerting, she unbuttoned and removed his shirt. At the gentle push of her hand he fell back onto the bed. She began to deftly work at cleaning and assessing his wounds. 'You're not too bad off,' she said. 'Not too much skin tore up. Mostly bruised a lot. You put up a good fight against those three.'

'Not good enough,' he lamented. 'I ain't took that good a beatin' for a long, long time.'

'You'd have gotten worse if Griff hadn't stepped in.'

'Who is he?'

She shrugged. 'He's just Griff. Used to work for Cambden. Didn't like his high-handed ways. He's Irish, after all. Like me. Anyway, he quit

73

and went to work for McDermott. That's what started the friction between Cambden and McDermott. Cambden gave McDermott orders not to hire Griff, and he did anyway.'

Levi winced as she cleaned a particularly deep wound. 'Does Cambden think he can even tell the other ranchers who to hire?'

Her voice betrayed her bitterness. 'He thinks he can tell everyone else everything they can do,' she said. 'And if they don't do as he says, they get whipped or run out of the country or killed.'

'What about McDermott?'

'Hiram McDermott,' she explained. 'He runs the Half Circle H, north of town. It's almost as big as Cambden's place, but he doesn't keep as many hands. He's a good man. Honest as the day is long. Tough enough to tell Cambden to go jump in the lake and get away with it.'

She rose and took the basin of water, now blood red, and dumped it in a commode. She refilled it with clean water and returned to the bed. Working swiftly and skillfully, she finished cleaning Levi's face and hands. She went to the dresser and removed a jar of some kind of ointment. She smeared it into each of the open wounds.

'Ouch!' Levi complained. 'That stuff smarts.'

'Oh, stop being a baby,' she teased. 'It'll keep them from putrefying, and make them heal faster.'

'What is it?'

She shrugged. 'Just some stuff my husband once used. I kept it. He put it on the cows' tits when they got chapped and cracked.'

'You were married?'

Her lips pulled together. Creases appeared at the corners of her mouth. Her voice went flat. 'I was till he crossed Cambden. Then he had an accident, and a horse that was so gentle little kids could crawl around his feet supposedly drug him to death. I had to let our homestead go, and nobody in the country would give me a job but Paddie. I didn't have money enough to go anywhere else, so here I am.'

'Tough way for a woman to make a livin'.'

She shrugged again. 'There's worse, I guess. I don't have to stay on my feet all day. Anyway, you lay down and try to get some sleep. I'll bring you up some supper after while. You can stay here a night or two.'

Levi's face telegraphed his hesitance. 'Don't worry,' she said. 'I'm not going to attack you, or sully your reputation.'

'I, no, I, it isn't that,' he protested. 'I don't want you to, well, what if Cambden finds out you're taking care of me?'

'Let him,' she said. She dumped the second basin of water into the commode and walked out of the room.

Levi needed to think through his situation. He needed to plan his next move. He needed to get to the hotel, to his own room. He just couldn't force himself up out of the bed. He told himself he'd worry about it all later. Then he let the bank of darkness hovering there close over him, blanking away the throbbing pain.

6

'And just what do you think you are doing?'

'Gettin' up. If I can.'

Connie glared at Levi. Hands on her hips, she leaned forward slightly. 'You are in no shape to be getting out of bed. You just get right back in that bed.'

Levi grinned. 'Sorry, Mother. I just gotta get movin'.'

Laugh wrinkles at the corners of her mouth betrayed Connie's stern appearance. 'I am not your mother, and just what do you have to do that's so important you can't give yourself at least a couple days in bed to heal? It's only been one whole day and part of another, you know. Now get back into bed.'

Levi cringed as he fought his stiff fingers to button his shirt. 'I'd like to, believe me. Especially with this care I'm gettin'. I ain't been fussed over like this since I was a kid.'

'Well, maybe you should be.'

'It could get to be a habit,' he admitted. 'What's happenin' around town?'

She shrugged. 'Not much. Lige has put out the word that no woman will be allowed to vote on the sixth.'

'And how are people reacting?'

Her chin tilted up. 'With a lot more gumption than I ever thought they would. Even the businessmen around town are saying that's not right. I've never seen or heard this town dare to talk against Cambden, or even disagree with him, before. It's almost scary.'

Levi nodded. He regretted it immediately. He held still, to allow the room to stop spinning. Connie spoke again. 'So where are you going?'

He looked at her a long moment. Finally he decided to trust her. 'I'm going to ride out to see McDermott, I'm going to ask him to be an election

79

judge, and to have some of his hands stay in town the whole day to ensure the election.'

'You're trying to start a range war.'

He frowned thoughtfully. 'I hope not. I also need to appoint a town marshal to take Slim Collins's place.'

She answered with no hesitation, as though she had been waiting for him to say that. 'How about Griff?'

His eyebrows shot up. 'Mulgrew?'

She nodded. 'He's as honest and dependable as they come. He's big enough and tough enough not many would try to stand up to him. And he needs a job.'

Levi studied her face. 'Do I hear some extra concern there somewhere?'

He was surprised at the blush that crept up her cheeks. 'Griff is a good man,' she protested. 'And he deserves a chance.'

'I thought he was working for McDermott.'

'Not any more, he's not. He was, but there's one of McDermott's hands he can't get along with. He quit so McDermott wouldn't be forced to fire one or the other of them.'

He thought it over. 'I'll see if I can find him.'

A smile played at the corners of her mouth. 'He's downstairs right now, waiting for you.'

'Why's he waiting for me?'

'Because I told him to wait there. I told him I thought you might want to offer him the job of town marshal.'

Half a dozen responses ran through Levi's head. Instead of any of them, he only grinned. He said, 'Do you already have the badge pinned on him too?'

She held out the town marshal's badge in her hand. 'No. But I did notice it in your pocket while you were sleeping, so I made sure you'd be able to find it when you went to talk to him.'

Levi's eyes twinkled. 'You wouldn't just happen to have designs on poor Griff, by any chance?'

'We've talked about it some,' she admitted.

'Poor Griff,' Levi said.

'Poor . . . ' she spluttered. 'Levi Hill! Do you want to find out what it feels like to get really hurt?'

He chuckled in spite of the pain it caused. 'Not me! I ain't afraid of Cambden's three toughest hands, but I ain't fool enough to fight an Irish lass.'

'Then get down there and give Griff an honest job so he can maybe afford to marry me and get me out of this place,' she said. 'And don't you dare tell him I said that!'

Levi hesitated at the door. 'I can give Griff the job, but only till next Tuesday. That job is up for election then, and he ain't even got his name on the ballot. Victoria Herder's runnin' for it too.'

Again, Connie's answer betrayed considerable thought that had already been given to the matter. 'She's running for Justice of the Peace, too. The same person shouldn't be both. Besides, a woman shouldn't be marshal anyway. And people could write Griff's name in, couldn't they? And if he does a good job, and if he helps you see to it that the election is fair, and if people see that he won't back down from Cambden, and if they're as fed up with him as I think they are, don't you think there's a really good chance they'd elect him to it? And if they elect him to the job, then Griff will know that the town thinks he's a good man, too. And then . . . '

Levi held up his hand against the torrent of words. 'Whoa, whoa! I'll ask him to be the town marshal for the time bein', but I ain't gettin' into all those what-ifs.'

She looked up at him, fighting tears back. His voice softened. 'You really do hate workin' here, don't you?'

She looked away. 'It's a living,' she said flatly. Then she turned back toward him. 'Yes! I do. I hate it. I hated it when I took the job, and I hate it even worse now. I hate selling my body to any drunk cowboy or soldier or whoever staggers into the bar with two dollars in his pocket. I hate the way I feel and smell and, and everything. But Griff has never treated me like a whore. He's treated me like a real lady. He's a good man, Levi.'

'Do you love him?'

She stared into the depths of nothing for several heartbeats. When she spoke her voice was soft. 'I like him. That's a start. I respect him, and he respects me, in spite of the way I make a living. I don't think I'll ever really love anyone, again. Not the way I did my husband. But I could spend my life with Griff, have his children, get old with him, and it would be good. I'm sure he'd always treat me good. Maybe that's not love, but that's more than most women in my profession could ever hope to have. I could be happy with that.'

He nodded. 'Does he love you?'

She nodded in return. 'Of course. A lonesome man doesn't need much to make him fall head over heels in love.

Men are awfully predictable that way, you know.'

'I don't know if I like that.'

Her eyes danced. 'You don't want to admit that women are stronger than men, and can wrap a man around their finger any time they want to?'

'Nope.'

'Well, get used to it. It's true, you know.'

'Then why did you say a woman shouldn't be marshal?'

She sobered at once. 'That's different. Women are stronger than men, emotionally. They show their emotions more, but they can control them better. But a woman can never be as big or as strong as a man. Being a marshal means handling a lot of drunk cowboys, things like that. A big man can handle them, lock them up if he needs to, and not hurt them. A woman couldn't. She'd either get hurt, or she'd have to hurt them. Or kill them. It just wouldn't work.'

He thought about it. 'That makes

sense. In fact, that pretty well reflects my own thinking.'

'Do you mean we agree?'

'Is that all that surprising?'

She wrinkled her nose at him. He said, 'Anyway, thank you for taking care of me the last couple days. I took quite a whipping.'

'I'd help anyone that stood up to Cambden and his bullies.'

He nodded and stepped from the room. He walked down the steps slowly. His eyes traveled warily around the room as he did. There was no indication of hostility directed toward him. He spotted Griff sitting at a table and walked toward him.

'Sure and look what staggered downstairs,' the big Irishman greeted him. 'You're lookin' like a herd of steers stampeded across your face, you are.'

Levi grinned in spite of the unwelcome movement of his sore and swollen face. 'I'd probably look a lot worse if you hadn't horned in when you did. I'm much obliged.'

'Sure an' I probably should have stepped in sooner, I should. It's just that I'm likin' to see a man fight 'is own fights as much as 'e can.'

Levi ignored the explanation. 'I hear you're in need of a job.'

'I am for a fact, I am.'

'Well, I'm in need of someone to appoint as town marshal, until the election. Are you interested?'

Griff looked around the room, then back to Levi. 'Are you thinkin' it might be workin' out the way the lass thinks it would?'

'I'd say there's a real good chance, anyway.'

'Then it's worth a shot, it is,' Griff responded at once. 'And sure 'twill be a welcome thing if Lige an' 'is boys come ridin' into town lookin' for a fight.'

Levi grinned painfully again. 'Here's your badge. I 'spect the jail keys and stuff are over at the marshal's office. I haven't even looked.'

'What are you about doin' now?'

'I'm going to ride out to McDermott's.

I'm going to ask him to be an election judge.'

'Are you thinkin' that's a smart thing? He's as certain as Lige is that it's a bad thing for women to be havin' the vote.'

Levi nodded. 'But if Connie's right, and she seems to have an awfully good sense of the people around here, he's also got a lot of integrity. I'm gambling his sense of honor and respect for the law will be stronger than his opinion of whether women should vote.'

Griff thought it over. 'It's a chance that you're right, it is. Well, if he doesn't shoot you, come on back to town. I'll be havin' the lid on the town waitin' for you. And if McDermott isn't wantin' to be involved in the election, there's MacLeash you could be askin'.'

'MacLeash?'

'Sure, an' Travis MacLeash is a neighbor of McDermott. He's in the next valley to the east, he is, an' as Scotch as McDermott but not strong against the women havin' the vote. He's a Scotchman, through an' through, but he's as honest an' well thought of as McDermott himself, he is.'

'I'll keep that in mind. There sure are a lot of Scotch and Irish in the same area here. I always heard they didn't get along.'

Griff grinned. 'That's a fact, when you're talkin' the Irish papists, it is. But there ain't a papist in the country. We're all shanty Irish around here. Sure an' the shanty Irish an' the Scotch is havin' no troubles gettin' along.'

Levi silently filed the information away for future reference. Some time it would come in handy to know that. He and Griff left the saloon together. Griff walked at once toward the marshal's office. Levi walked toward the livery barn to retrieve his horse. 'Gonna be a long ride, feelin' like this,' he reminded himself. 'I sure hope some of the soreness works itself out in a hurry. I couldn't whip my way out of a wet paper bag the way I feel right now.'

7

'Good one, Tommy! You got 'im right in the ribs!'

The dog's yelp, coming right before the boy's exuberant yell, made it all too evident what was happening. Levi pulled the reins, frowning. He turned Blue into the space between two buildings along Cambden's main street. As he emerged behind the row of stores, his eyes narrowed.

A large yellow dog was cornered against a board fence. Five boys, ranging in age from ten to fourteen were lined up in a half circle. Each had a handful of rocks. They were taking turns throwing them at the dog.

When one of the boys walked in too close, the dog growled and showed his teeth, forcing him to back away. Otherwise, he made no effort to attack the boys. His tail was pulled between his legs. His head was low. He whined intermittently, as though pleading for mercy.

Unseen by the boys, Levi dismounted. His sore and swollen lips were pressed painfully together. He took his lariat from his saddle. He uncoiled three loops of rope, providing about six feet of strong, stiff rope. He walked up behind the boys. Swinging the end of the rope like a whip, he lashed across the nearest boy's buttocks.

The boy let out a yell. He dropped his rocks and grabbed his backside. Whirling, he saw Levi, already swinging the rope again. He fled, yelling, both hands clinging to his stinging rear.

The other boys were too intent on their own yelling and watching the cornered animal to even notice. The second boy jumped straight in the air when the rope lashed his rump. His mouth opened wide, but no sound emitted. He landed, spotted Levi, and fled, without making any noise whatever.

The third boy screamed in pain when the rope connected. That caught the attention of the other two boys. The three turned in fear, facing Levi, backing slowly away. The boy who had last felt the wrath of the rope clutched his backside. Tears streamed down his face.

'What do you think you're doing to that poor dog?' Levi yelled at them.

Cringing in fear, the three backed against the fence they had trapped the dog against. As Levi advanced, the dog appeared suddenly between him and the boy. All sign of timidity was gone. His ears were laid back tight against his head. The hair on his neck and back stood straight up. His lips were pulled back from his teeth. He snarled threateningly at Levi.

Levi stopped and took a step backward. 'Whoa!' he said. 'Does this dog belong to one of you?'

The boys looked at one another, then back at Levi. Nobody spoke. Levi spoke again, 'I asked if this was your dog.'

The oldest of the boys — he couldn't have been more than eleven — said, 'No, sir, mister. He's just a stray. He don't belong to nobody.'

'Then why were you throwing rocks at him?'

The three looked at each other, then at the ground. The spokesman finally said, 'I dunno. It just seemed kinda funny.'

'Would you think it was kinda funny if someone had you cornered, throwing rocks at you?'

They didn't answer. He pursued it. 'Do you think it's funny now, being backed up against that fence from my rope, just waitin' to see how much it's going to hurt? Is that funny?'

The three shook their heads, staring at him now in wide-eyed fear. 'You back that poor dog up against the fence and pelt him with rocks, and when I stop you, he stands there and tries to protect you from me! Don't that make you plumb ashamed of yourselves?'

The three stared at the ground again.

Levi said, 'You boys get out of here! And don't you ever pull a stunt like that again, you hear?'

After an instant's hesitation, the three ran like the banshee was on their tails. As soon as they were gone, the dog's demeanor changed. His tail dropped, then stayed tucked between his legs. He changed instantly from a threatening posture to a pleading one. He licked his lips, bobbing his head.

'You are some strange dog,' Levi said.

At the sound of his voice, the dog's tail shot out from between his legs and began to wag. He took a hesitant step toward Levi and stopped. Levi dropped to one knee and held out a hand. 'Well, come here, then.'

Slowly the dog inched forward, sampling the air continually. When he could barely reach it, he extended his nose to sniff Levi's extended hand. Satisfied, he took another step forward. Levi scratched under the dog's neck gently. The dog responded by rubbing the side of his nose on Levi's arm.

'Hey, I like that! You don't even try to lick,' Levi crooned.

The dog responded to the sound of his voice at once. He walked forward and rubbed the side of his head on Levi's leg. Levi began to pet him, exploring his thick, curly hair. 'Boy, you're a mess, dog,' he said. 'You got enough burrs and stuff in your hide to plant a bramble patch. You don't seem to have fleas, though. You could stand a square meal or two, too. If it wasn't for that thick coat of hair, I could count your ribs from across the street. You suppose we could maybe find you something to eat?'

The dog stood still, wagging his tail slowly, relishing the unaccustomed attention. After a few minutes Levi stood. 'Well, I ain't got time to mess with you, dog. You better go scrounge up a meal somewhere.'

He turned and mounted Blue, coiling and replacing his lariat. He rode back between the buildings, into the street and out of town. At the edge of town he turned and looked back. The big yellow dog was trotting along just behind Blue. Levi stopped. 'Hey, dog. You don't want to go following me. There ain't much dog food where I'm going.'

The dog sat down in the road and stared at him. Levi turned and nudged Blue back into motion. Glancing over his shoulder he noticed the dog had resumed following him. He shrugged. 'He'll turn back after a bit, I 'spect,' he mumbled.

Five or six miles out of town the dog still followed. They had climbed steadily along the course of a mountain stream. A rabbit darted out of a clump of brush. Turning Blue sideways to the running animal, Levi's hand streaked to his gun. As the forty-five leaped from the holster it barked once. The rabbit somersaulted high in the air and landed without moving.

The dog leaped forward, running with his belly to the ground. Levi's mouth opened to protest, then he closed it again. The dog skidded to a halt at the dead rabbit. He picked it up and turned, trotting back to Levi. He dropped it at Blue's front feet, backed up a couple steps, and sat down, looking at Levi and panting happily.

'Well what d'ya know!' Levi breathed. 'As hungry as you gotta be, and you brought the rabbit to me! Somebody's taught you really good!'

He dismounted and cleaned the rabbit. He skinned it, head and all. Then he cut off the head and removed the entrails, tossing them aside. The dog wolfed them down eagerly. 'Guess we'd just as well stop and eat a bite,' Levi said.

Building a small fire, he positioned the rabbit over the flames to cook. As it did, he made a pot of coffee with water from the stream. He dug some dried biscuits from his saddle-bags. He picked some blackberries from bushes along the stream. When the rabbit was done he squatted down and ate nearly half of it. The dog sat, watching the whole time. He made no effort to take any of the food except what Levi tossed to him. Whatever bones, pieces of biscuit, or the remainder of the rabbit that Levi threw to him, he gulped down as if he were starving.

When he was finished, Levi repacked his things. He carefully put out the fire, and mounted. The dog fell into place behind him.

They had ridden nearly another mile when the dog suddenly growled quietly. Levi jerked Blue to a stop. The dog was staring in the direction they were travelling. His ears were laid back. The hair on his back stood straight up. Levi listened intently, but could hear nothing. The dog growled again.

Looking around, Levi spotted a thick clump of brush and trees. He turned Blue into them, moving back out of sight, then turning where he could watch the clearing they had just left. The dog came and lay down silently beside him.

Less than five minutes went by before Levi heard a pair of horses coming. Almost as soon as he heard them, two riders emerged from the timber. It was Tug Wilson and John Dally, two of the men who had beaten him up a couple days before. They were talking, paying no attention to their surroundings. Levi resisted the urge to act. He took a measure of satisfaction from their black eyes, the swelling and discoloration of their faces, but he knew his own looked even worse. He sat his horse in silence as they rode on through the clearing.

He started to move Blue out of the trees. The dog growled again. Levi stopped. The dog stayed where he had been. Levi started to speak. The dog growled softly again. Levi frowned. Just as he was about to speak again, another rider emerged from the timber. It was the third man of the trio from the saloon. He was riding at a trot, apparently to catch up with his comrades.

When the third man had disappeared, the dog rose from his place and trotted into the clearing. 'I'll say one thing,' Levi said as he followed, 'you do have good ears.'

It was late afternoon when Levi arrived at the Half Circle H ranch. Hiram McDermott stepped outside to see what his dogs were barking at as he rode into the yard. 'Get down and come in,' he called. 'You're just in time for supper.'

'Thanks,' Levi responded. 'Don't mind if I do.'

'You can put your horse in the barn and give him a bait of oats if you like, then come on in,' the rancher invited. 'You'd be Levi Hill, I guess.'

Levi stopped in his tracks. 'How'd you know that?'

'You might say your face gave it away,' the rancher grinned. 'News gets around fast in this country. Along with a pretty good description, I'll admit.'

Levi grinned through stiff and swollen

lips. 'I 'spect news moves faster'n I do today.'

'Where'd you pick up the dog?'

Levi looked at the yellow dog, busy making an uneasy peace with the rancher's three dogs. 'In town. I stopped some kids from throwin' rocks at him, and he seems to have adopted me.'

'You could do worse,' the rancher said. 'He belonged to one o' the hands at the Double J. He was teachin' the dog to be a cow dog, and he had the makin's of a good 'un.'

'Something happen to him?'

'He got killed.'

Levi waited for the rest of the story, but it wasn't forthcoming. Instead of prying he said, 'Why didn't somebody take the dog?'

'He wouldn't go with anybody. Just hung around town. I'm surprised he took up with you. Well, take care of your horse and we'll talk over supper.'

An hour later, with his stomach comfortably full, Levi leaned back to give full attention to his coffee. Deliah McDermott said, 'We've heard an awful lot about you, Mr Hill. It isn't often we have a celebrity stop in.'

Levi was instantly uncomfortable. 'I've never thought of myself as any kind of celebrity,' he protested.

'What brings you out this way?' McDermott interjected, deliberately rescuing Levi from his discomfort.

Levi took a deep breath and plunged in. 'You. You have the reputation of a good man, tough, fair and honest.'

'Now you're the one pilin' on the blarney.'

'Just bein' honest with why I'm here. I 'spect you already know I'm a Pinkerton man.'

Both the rancher and his wife nodded, so he continued. 'I was sent here because of the election coming up next week. I'm sure you know Victoria Herder's runnin' for office. Since it's the first time women have had the right to vote, and since she's runnin', they sent me up here to see that nobody messes with the election, and nobody tries to get rid of her.'

'What does that have to do with me?'

'I need somebody to be the election judge in town. Somebody has to run the election, make sure it's fair, nobody votes twice, everybody that wants to vote gets to, and the votes are counted honestly.'

McDermott shook his head. 'You're barkin' up the wrong tree. In the first pace, I ain't in favor of the whole deal at all. I never thought women oughta have the vote, an' I sure as . . . I sure don't think no woman oughta run for no office. Especially marshal! I don't know who might've told you I'd be interested in makin' it happen.'

Levi grinned. 'Nobody told me you were in favor of it. In fact, that's one of the reasons I wanted you.' His grin faded as he continued. 'The whole country knows you don't like the idea. But the same people tell me you've got a lot of integrity, and you're a man that goes by the law. To be honest, I don't like the whole idea either. I don't mind women voting. That seems to me to be a matter of intelligence and judgment, and women are just as smart as men. Most of the time they're a better instinctive judge of character. But I don't like the idea of a woman holding office. But what I like is beside the point. It's the law. Either we obey the law, and uphold the law, even the laws we don't like and don't agree with, or we're no different from any other outlaws. Even the worst of men obey the laws they agree with.'

McDermott pulled out his tobacco and rolled a cigarette thoughtfully. When he had it lighted, he exhaled a cloud of smoke. He said, 'I guess I agree, up to a point. I wouldn't fight against the law, the way Cambden says he's going to. I just can't see why it oughta be my duty to stick my neck out to support a law I don't agree with.'

Levi sighed. 'Because if you don't, or if somebody doesn't, then Cambden will get away with being above the law. He'll be in a position of telling the whole country what laws they can obey and what ones they can't. Law abiding men can't let that happen.'

McDermott smoked the rest of his cigarette in silence. He snuffed out the butt in his plate. 'Well, you make a good case, I'll say that for you. You may even be right. What do you think, Deliah?'

Deliah spoke as if she were just waiting to be asked. 'I think he's right, Hiram, but I'm afraid. If you do, you'll be putting yourself squarely against Lige. He's not a man to take that kindly. It might even cause a range war.'

McDermott considered her words for a long moment. Levi resisted the urge to speak, letting the man have the time to think it through.

He stood abruptly. 'All right,' he said simply. 'There might be hell to pay, but it's the right thing to do. I'll come into town on Sunday and get things set up.

I'll bring all my boys along. I don't suppose there'd be any way to get them deputized or something, would there?'

'I'm sure that wouldn't be any problem,' Levi assured him. 'I'll just ask Griff to do that.'

The rancher's eyebrows shot up. 'Griff?'

Levi grinned. 'Oh, there's something the grapevine didn't get here with yet! Griff Mulgrew is the town marshal until after the election.

'On whose say-so? What happened to Slim?'

'On my say-so. By my authority from the territorial governor, I relieved Slim of his office and put Griff in as marshal.'

McDermott grinned broadly. 'Boy, I bet Lige is fit to be tied over that!'

'Lige ain't too happy about a lot of things right now,' Levi agreed.

Deliah broke in. 'If you're going to be the election judge, are you going to let me vote?'

McDermott's face turned bright red.

He opened his mouth twice and shut it silently each time. Finally he said, 'Well, I guess I can't be two-faced enough to take a job makin' sure any other woman in the country can vote if I won't even let my own wife vote. But if you vote for that Herder woman for marshal, I'll . . . '

'You'll never know,' Deliah grinned. 'Secret ballots, remember?'

McDermott turned to Levi. 'You see what kinda problems this sorta thing's causin' already?'

There were far worse problems Levi could envision. He was fully aware most of them would be more than idle worry.

8

'Well, dog, I think Hiram's gonna do a great job,' Levi told the animal waiting expectantly for him to complete saddling Blue. His square nose and blocky face watched Levi expectantly. His oversized ears were perked forward as far as their weight would allow. His tail, with its patches of too-long hair and patches of near baldness, wagged slowly from side to side.

Levi stopped and looked at the dog. He laughed suddenly. 'You are about the ugliest dog I ever saw,' he grinned. 'You look like you're somewhere between two and twelve, and that cowboy had to've fed you ugly pills for the first six months you were alive.'

The dog bobbed his head, delighted to hear Levi's voice, oblivious to the meaning of the words. His tail kept its rhythmic wag.

A sudden thought occurred to Levi. He turned away from his horse and walked back to the yard. Hiram McDermott was just entering the corral, his lariat in his hand. He stopped when he saw Levi's approach. 'I never thought to ask,' Levi said, 'You don't happen to know what that cowpoke that got killed called this dog, do you? I ain't figured out his name.'

McDermott stopped and stared thoughtfully for a long moment. His eyes lighted up abruptly. 'Curly!' he said. 'I'm pertneart sure he called him Curly.'

'That fits,' Levi said. 'Much obliged.'

As though both men understood the conversation was finished, and both had more important things to do, they both turned and walked away from each other without another word. Half-way to the barn Levi called, 'Curly!'

The big yellow dog bounded out of the horse barn. His ears flopped up and down in rhythm with his awkward-looking gait. His tongue lolled out the side of his mouth. He bounded to within two steps of Levi, then set all four feet and skidded to a halt. He snapped his mouth shut with an audible click. He sat as still as he could manage, squirming in anticipation, but remaining in a sitting position as he had obviously been so well trained to do. Levi laughed again. He reached down and rubbed the dog's head. 'Well, Curly, I guess we know your name, don't we?'

Curly's head jerked around. His tail came up. He stared intently toward the road. Levi turned to see what had arrested the dog's attention. A lone rider was just entering the yard. McDermott had seen him as well. Leading the horse he had just roped, he stepped over beside Levi and waited his arrival.

'Howdy, Tim,' McDermott greeted the rider.

'Mornin' Mr McDermott,' the rider

responded. 'Fine mornin'.'

' 'Tis for a fact. What's on your mind this mornin'?'

'Well, I was purty close here, checkin' on some steers, so I thought I'd stop by an' ask if you was hirin'.'

The old rancher looked Tim over carefully. 'Well,' he drawled, 'I might be. Ain't you workin' for MacLeash?'

'Yup. Been workin' fer 'im nigh onto a year an' a half.'

'Why are you lookin' for a different job? MacLeash pays the same as the rest of us, don't he?'

Tim nodded his head. 'I just gotta get me a different job.'

'MacLeash didn't can you, did he?'

'No, he ain't canned me. But I'm fixin' to turn in my time, an' bein' a married man I gotta find me a different job afore I do.'

The rancher looked thoughtful. 'Well, I could use a hand all right. I'm partial to married hands when I can get 'em. But I don't make a practice of hiring guys out from under one of my neighbors.'

'Oh, that there ain't no problem,' Tim assured him. 'MacLeash knows I'm a-lookin'. Fact is, he done tol' me I'd oughta find me a different outfit to work for.'

The rancher's eyebrows shot up. 'That a fact? Why'd he do that, without firin' you?'

Tim looked uncomfortable. 'Well, fact is, I just ain't good enough to work for MacLeash. I'm a fair to middlin' cowboy, but I ain't real awful good. I'm steady an' honest, an' I don't drink or nothin'. I don't go whorin' around when I go to town. I'm a good solid married man, with two kids, an' happy with it. But MacLeash, he gets an awful lot outa his hands. Fact is, he wants more outa his hands than I got in me to give.'

'I've heard he gets a lot out of his hands,' the rancher agreed.

'He does that for a fact,' Tim affirmed. 'An' he's got some o' the best cowpokes I ever seen a-workin' fer him. Why, there's some o' them boys what get more work done afore breakfast than I can get done all day long. An' I just ain't got it in me to ever be that good. I know it, an' MacLeash knows it. There ain't no bad blood between us or nothin'. He just don't never keep too many hands on 'is payroll, an' he thinks he's gotta get a awful lot outa the hands he does keep.'

'Would forty a month do you?' McDermott asked. 'I'll furnish your beef and all the usual stuff. I'll furnish you two milk cows so that your kids'll have milk, if you do the milkin' and split the milk with the cookhouse. You can run up to two dozen o' your own cows on my place, no cost to you. You can add up to ten cows each year you stay with me. I'll furnish you five horses, and you can use a ranch buggy or wagon to go to town when you need to. But I'll expect you to be on the job the same time as the rest o' the hands, and work just as hard.'

Tim grinned like he'd just been handed an early Christmas present. 'Oh, I'll sure do that, Mr McDermott,' he beamed. 'I'll sure do that. You won't be sorry you hired me. An' if your cook needs help or somethin', the missus is a real hand in the kitchen. She'll be plumb happy to help out, an' won't charge you nothin' neither.'

Silently McDermott pulled off his glove and extended a hand. Tim gripped it excitedly. 'Is one o' them houses over there fer yer married hands?' he pointed.

McDermott nodded. 'You can have the far one. It's the only one empty. You can move in whenever you want, and we'll start you then.'

'Well, OK. Thanks again. You won't be sorry.'

'You'll be going back to the ranch now? To MacLeash's, I mean.'

'Yessir.'

'Tell Travis for me that I'll be runnin' the election in town on Tuesday. Tell him I'd be obliged if he'd help out, and to bring all the hands he can spare.'

'Is that a fact?' Tim marveled. 'You're runnin' the election! Well I'll be . . . well, yeah. I'll tell him. I sure will. Well, thanks again . . . boss.' He whirled his horse and headed out of the yard at a gallop.

Levi mounted and left the yard as well. The dog fell into place about a horse's length behind him.

9

Levi squirmed in the saddle. He tried to find a comfortable position. There was none. The effect of his beating refused to go away that quickly. 'At least I had a good bed at McDermott's,' he consoled himself. Both horse and dog disdained to answer.

They rode all day, circling toward Victoria Herder's place. They stopped for the night along another swiftly flowing stream. Levi picked a spot carefully, a hundred yards from the stream, against a tall cliff. Thick brush and deadfall timber made approach to his campsite in silence impossible. It was unlikely anyone looking for him would even spot it. He picketed Blue in a lush stand of grass twenty yards to his right.

He shot a pair of mountain quail for supper, feeding both himself and his dog before turning in. He slept soundly until the low rumble in the dog's throat wakened him. The sky was just lightening in the east, promising dawn.

He listened intently for the source of the dog's warning, and heard nothing. He slipped silently into his boots. He checked his forty-five and dropped it into his holster, then put on his coat against the bite of the pre-dawn chill. He still heard nothing. From time to time, however, Curly issued another low growl of warning.

Walking silently, Levi retrieved his horse. In the increasing light, he rolled up his bedroll, packed his things, and saddled Blue. When everything was loaded and ready, he stopped again to listen. He still heard nothing. Then, just as he was about to decide the dog was wrong, he heard a branch break a ways downstream. He froze, listening. A few minutes later he heard a bear snort and grouse softly.

Levi relaxed. 'Heard a bear, huh?'

he whispered to his dog. 'You woke me up for a bear? Well, let's have a look at him.'

Mounting Blue he moved slowly and silently in the direction he had heard the bear. He had ridden about three hundred yards when he came to the edge of the timber. Stretched before him was a large clearing, possibly five hundred yards across. He could see no sign of the bear.

As he sat there in the trees, Curly growled again. Levi glanced at the animal. He was looking across the clearing, downstream.

Almost as soon as he looked that way, Levi spotted a horse's head. The horse moved into sight, following some slight trail he hadn't even noticed. It was John Dally. 'Him again!' Levi breathed.

Right behind Dally, Tug Wilson and the other cowboy, whose name Levi still didn't know, followed.

'I still don't see why we need to get back so danged early,' Tug complained.

'It wasn't supposed to take us all day to get them heifers over there,' John reminded him. 'The boss wants us back today so we can start tryin' to bust up that election.'

'I ain't real sure I even wanta do that,' the third man observed.

'What'sa matter, Will?' Tug grinned. 'Losin' yer appetite for tanglin' with that Pinkerton guy?'

'Well, I don't look forward to it, that's for sure,' Will admitted. 'But I ain't sure it's right anyway. I ain't never bucked the law. I ain't sure I can keep workin' for Lige if it's gonna mean doin' that.'

The other two were strangely silent for a long moment. They were almost even with Levi's vantage point when John said, 'Yeah, I know what you mean. We either gotta back 'im or find another job, though. I ain't gonna let 'im down as long as I'm takin' his pay.'

'Hey!' Tug said. 'What's that?'

The three reined in abruptly. Levi's

119

hand dropped to his gun, but they were looking forward, not toward him. He followed their gaze, aware of Curly's low growl again. As he looked, a huge grizzly lumbered out of the timber about fifty yards ahead of the trio. He stopped and stared at them. A low, rumbling growl issued from his throat.

'Wow!' John said. 'Look at the size of that bugger!'

'He's a grizzly, too,' Tug agreed. 'I don't like grizzlies. You ain't never got no idea what they're gonna do. He might run in a minute, or he might just come after us.'

Will said, 'What'sa matter, Tug? You scared of 'im? I always thought you said you could rope anything with hair on his belly. That there bear's sure got plenty hair on his belly. Let's see you rope 'im.'

'Are you nuts?' John replied. 'That's a grizzly. He'd turn around and come right after you if you tried.'

'Not if I heeled 'im,' Will argued.

'What? Are you serious?'

'I'm dead serious,' Will said. 'I always wanted to try to rope a bear. I can't see why we couldn't, if Tug heads 'im and we both heel 'im. He sure ain't no stronger'n a big bull. If we stretch 'im out, he can't even chew on the ropes.'

The bear growled louder, tossing his head. A long string of white saliva trailed from his mouth as he tossed his head. 'He's gettin' mad at us, just sittin' here,' Tug observed. 'We'd best do somethin', or he'll be comin' after us.'

'You boys game to try this?' John asked.

'Dang right!' Will said.

'Aw, why not?' Tug agreed. 'Cain't do no worse'n get kilt.'

The three grabbed for their lariats. They shook out their loops, and Tug nudged his horse forward. The animal snorted and pranced. His ears laid back tight against his head. Tug did not crowd him hard, but he kept nudging him forward. 'C'mon buck,' he coaxed. 'Go get him!'

Finally the horse responded. He saw the loop of Tug's lariat begin to whirl, and knew what he was being asked to do. Ears still pinned back tight to his head, he began to run toward the bear. Even as he ran, he whined his fear.

John and Will followed, loops whirling. Will's horse squealed in fear, but ran straight toward the huge grizzly.

The bear took a step backward, clearly baffled by the cowboy's behavior. He was accustomed to everything running away from him, not toward him. He turned and started to lumber away. He had gone no more than three or four steps when Tug's loop settled over his head. Tug's horse set his feet, and the noose tightened around the bear's neck.

Jerked around by the strange and unexpected bond around his neck, the bear roared his surprise and rage. He tried to rear up on his hind legs, but the back-pedaling horse jerked him back to all fours instantly.

Circling the bear, Will threw a loop that turned over right in front of the bear's hind leg. While the loop was still in the air, the forward drag of the other rope forced the bear to step forward, putting his hind foot right into the loop. Will's horse stopped instantly and began to back. Will jerked the rope tight and dallied it around his saddle horn, lifting the bear's hind leg off the ground.

The bear roared again and tried to whirl, snapping at the strange thing gripping his back leg. The rope around his neck kept him from doing so. He tried to turn back to snap at the rope leading from his neck. Just as he did, John's loop closed around his other hind leg.

The two horses pulling backward, one attached to each hind leg, and the other horse pulling forward, attached to his neck, stretched the huge bear helplessly on the ground. 'We got 'im!' Will whooped. 'We got that sucker stretched out like a yearlin' steer!'

The other two laughed and hollered in a combination of fear and exultation. 'I didn't think we could do it,' John admitted.

'I told you I could rope anything that had hair on its belly!' Tug replied.

The three laughed again. They slapped their legs, sending dust clouding up from their chaps. The laughter slowly died away. The three sat their horses, watching the bear, still roaring his defiance, snapping his huge jaws. Almost as one, the three sighed and shook their heads. It was Will who finally spoke. 'Well, we got 'im. Now what are we gonna do with 'im?'

The silence that followed his words was broken only by the bear's furious growls and roars, and the frightened snorting of the horses. Levi felt a swell of admiration for those horses. Locked in the grip of fear such as they were, they still responded to their training, keeping the ropes tight, keeping their riders safe. They would do so, he knew, as long as they were called upon to.

'Let's brand 'im!' John yelled suddenly.

'What?'

'That's what we rope critters for, ain't it?' John argued. 'We got 'im roped. Let's slap a C bar C on 'im. We'll be the only outfit in the country with a grizzly bear wearin' the outfit's brand.'

Will bailed off of his horse. 'I'll build a fire!' he said.

'I got an iron with a cinch ring on the end for brandin',' Tug responded.

The other two dismounted as well, hurrying to help Will gather wood for a fire. As they quickly built the fire, Levi moved back into the trees, circling to a better vantage point. He could hear the bear, alternately in fear and rage, growling, snarling and struggling as the fire was built less than three feet from where he lay stretched helplessly.

When the fire was ready, the cowboys heated the simple branding iron, made with an iron ring welded to the end of an iron rod. By heating the ring, they could use it to 'write' any brand desired on the hide of a cow or calf. Or, in this case, an angry bear.

When it was hot, John grabbed the iron and began to draw a large C on the bear's side. As the hot iron hit his hide, the bear howled and roared in fear and pain, redoubling his efforts to break the ropes or reach them to chew them in two. The horses snorted in fear. They were jerked and yanked. They planted their feet better and leaned back, holding their steady pressure against the ropes. Confident of their mounts, the cowboys watched in rapt awe as John made the C on the bear's side.

By the time the C was complete, the iron was too cool to continue. He returned the iron to the fire to reheat it. 'I get to do the next part,' Will said.

'Then I'll do the other C,' Tug agreed. 'I can't wait till we tell the boys what we did.'

'I ain't sure we better tell Lige,' John said.

'What? Why not?'

'We're supposed to be gettin' back quick, remember? You wanta tell Lige you was killin' time brandin' a grizzly bear?'

'Killin' time?' Will protested. 'Whatd'ya mean, killin' time? This here's the dangest thing any cowpokes have ever done in this country. This ain't killin' time. Ever' outfit in the country'll be talkin' about this at roundup ever' year for years an' years to come.'

'Tell Lige that,' John responded.

The silence that followed attested to the weight of the argument. Will grabbed the branding iron and drew a horizontal line for the bar that would mark the space between the two Cs. The bear convulsed in new paroxysms of rage and pain. The ropes did not yield. Will put the iron back in the hottest part of the fire.

'He didn't squawk quite as hard that time,' Will observed.

'Gotta be your tender touch on the brandin' iron,' Tug teased.

'I told you I was good,' Will responded.

They waited until the iron was red hot again, and Tug grabbed it. The three were so rapt in watching they failed to notice the bear had squirmed around enough to get the rope that extended from around his neck between his teeth. He was chewing furiously on it. Levi saw what was happening, and grabbed his own lariat. He hit Blue with his spurs and shot from the trees, already whirling his loop.

Tug finished with the final C and started to step back as the rope snapped. The bear whirled toward the three, lashing out with his front feet and snapping his huge jaws. As they yelled and recoiled in terror, only the ropes on the bear's hind feet spared their lives. The other two horses, responding to the lessening pressure on the ropes, began to walk backward, keeping the ropes tight, dragging the angry bruin backward.

The bear whirled to attack the ropes on his hind feet as the three cowboys sprinted for their horses. Only as they leaped into their saddles did they see Levi. His loop was just settling over the bear's head as they whirled to look. Blue skidded to a halt and began backing.

The loop tightened around the bear's neck. He squealed in fury at the replacement of a restraint he had just conquered, and whirled to fight it. The three ropes once again snapped taut, however, and he was once more helplessly stretched on the ground. His fury could be vented only in roars that sent chills down the back of men and animals alike. Froth ringed his mouth.

'Hill!' John exclaimed.

The other two just stared in disbelief at the man they had beaten so badly four days before.

'Nice job of brandin',' Levi said quietly. 'Now how are you boys gonna get your ropes back, without that bear killin' you?'

The three stared, open-mouthed. None of the trio offered to answer the question they hadn't even thought to ask.

10

'Forget the ropes,' Tug said. 'I ain't tryin' to get 'em back.'

The other three stared with him at the furious animal on the ground. The bear, still helplessly stretched between the three lariats, was so furious he was out of his mind. He frothed at the mouth, twisted, roared and fought relentlessly against his restraints. His strength was such that the horses were continually dragged forward by his pull on the rope, fighting their way back again as they just as continually stretched him full length again.

'What are you doin' here?' John asked Levi.

'Oh, just watchin' you boys havin' fun,' Levi said. 'Till I saw him get that rope in his mouth. I was afraid he'd kill you boys before you could get away from him, then.'

Will frowned. 'You risked your neck to dab a rope on him, just to save us, after what we done to you the other night?'

'I never was too smart,' Levi grinned. He noticed with satisfaction that it didn't hurt quite so much to grin. The swelling must have fairly well begun to leave his lips.

'Now that takes a real man,' Tug said. Awe tinged his voice. 'We're much obliged, Hill.'

Uncomfortable with the direction of the conversation, Levi brought it back to reality. 'So how do you fine cowboys figure to get your ropes back? My rope too, as a matter of fact.'

'Forget 'em,' Tug repeated. 'They ain't worth it. Turn 'im loose and run for all we're worth. Then we can come back an' get our ropes after he's gone off somewheres.'

'I ain't leavin' my lariat!' John argued. 'I already had to ask Lige for two new ones in the last month. That big ol' bull busted one, and that mad cow that I didn't get dallied quick enough got off with another one, an' I never could find it. If I go back an' say, 'Oh, yeah, Lige, I need another new rope', do you know what he's gonna do to me?'

Will nodded. 'Dang right I do. He used that bull whip o' his on me once. He's meaner than a rattlesnake when he's mad.'

'He ain't never used the bull whip on me,' Tug said, 'but he had the boys chap me one winter when we was stayin' in a line shack. It was colder'n blazes, an' we'd been eatin' a lot o' beans, an' I broke wind inside, 'stead o' goin' outside first. It was pretty rank, I'll admit. He got plumb mad about it, and had 'em hold me down an' whip me like a kid, usin' my chaps. I tell you that hurt worse'n anything I ever had did to me. You ain't never been whipped till you been chapped that-away.'

'That's what I mean,' John said. 'If you think I'm gonna go ask for another lariat, then have to tell 'im I let a grizzly bear have this one, you got another think comin'!'

'So what're we gonna do?' Will asked.

The three looked at Levi as though he ought to have the answer. He offered nothing except a grin. John said, 'Well, I got an idea, maybe. I got a thirty-thirty. I've heard tell a thirty-thirty won't go through a bear's skull. Epecially a grizzly. Maybe I could shoot him between the eyes. Not straight on, mind ya, but kinda at an angle. It'd glance off, most likely. It might not kill 'im. It might just knock 'im out. Then we could get our ropes off'n'im and get away from 'im afore he comes to.'

'What if it didn't work?' Tug asked. 'What if it killed him?'

John shrugged. 'What difference does it make? If it kills 'im, we won't have to worry about 'im killin' calves. We probably ought've killed him when we seen 'im anyway.'

Will shook his head. 'I didn't go through all this to get a brand on him, just to kill 'im. There ain't no sense in brandin' a dead bear. It ain't even funny if the brand ain't on a real live bear, runnin' around the country. Then everybody that sees 'im will know what we did. If he's dead, there ain't nobody ever even gonna know.'

Tug said, 'So have you got a better idea? I still say we turn 'im loose an' run for it. We can watch from the timber an' come back an' get our ropes.'

'As mad as he is?' John argued. 'He'll tear every one of them ropes up into little pieces. If he can't get ahold of us, he'll take it out on them till he ain't mad no more. That's gonna take a while. That there brand's gonna be plumb sore for a week or more, so it'll take him at least that long to stop bein' mad. If we let 'im have the ropes, we ain't gonna get nothin' but tore up hemp fuzz back when he's done.'

Silence descended again. Tug tipped

his hat forward, scratching the back of his head. John stroked the stubble on his jaw thoughtfully. Will stared at the bear, chuckling at his futile and impotent rage.

It was Levi who finally spoke. 'Any of you boys got a bottle?'

'This ain't no time to be drinkin',' John scolded. 'Anyway, I'd always heard you wasn't much of a drinkin' man.'

'Not for me,' Levi explained. 'If we had a bottle or two, we could probably get him drunk. His head's pretty well held in place. If Tug takes what's left of his lariat, that's already broke . . . '

'Yeah, but it's just the loop what he chewed off,' Tug interrupted. 'I'll just tie another honda on it, and nobody'll even know the difference. Lige always give us forty foot lariats anyway.'

Levi continued from where he had been interrupted. 'So take your lariat an' fix a new loop, so we can get a second loop on his neck. Then we can hold his head still enough to pour some whiskey down him. I've heard that after the first drink or two, a bear'll gulp it right down. If we can get him drunk enough, we could jerk the ropes off and get away while he's tryin' to stand up.'

The three looked at one another for a long moment. Tug whirled and sprinted to his horse. He quickly tied the knots to make another loop in his lariat. He tossed it over the bear's head. His horse instantly backed against it, tightening it.

The bear renewed the fury of his rage and resistance. 'I'd think he'd be gettin' a sore throat by now,' Will observed.

'Prob'ly is,' John agreed. 'That's just one more thing to make 'im mad.'

Tug reached into his saddle-bag. 'Here's a bottle,' he said. 'It's a quart. I ain't had but one nip out've it.'

'Who's gonna do it?' Will asked.

'Not me!' John said.

'Me neither!' Tug agreed. 'I'll furnish the bottle, but I ain't gettin' up there where he can get them claws on me.'

'I ain't either,' Will said.

Levi dismounted, grinning. He held his hand out to Tug, who passed him the bottle of whiskey as if it were hot. Levi walked around the bear, ducking under one of the lariats, keeping where the bear could not reach him with a front paw. He pulled the cork from the bottle. Extending his arm as far as possible, he sloshed whiskey into the gaping, snapping jaw of the bear.

The bear gagged and swallowed. He shook his head. He coughed. The four men laughed too loudly, betraying the level of their fear.

The grizzly opened his mouth to growl at Levi, fighting furiously to get his head turned around to where he could tear at him. Levi sloshed more of the whiskey into his gaping mouth.

This time the bear swallowed, then shook his head. He started to growl, then shook his head again. He turned to snarl at Levi, and got another, larger gulp of whiskey sloshed into his mouth.

This time the bear swallowed, then closed his mouth. He licked his lips and shook his head. He licked his lips again. He growled, but not as loudly, and twisted his head toward Levi again. As his mouth opened, Levi sloshed another jolt of whiskey into it.

The strange dance of bottle and bear continued until the bottle was dry. By the last third of the bottle, the bear almost appeared to be opening his mouth to receive the fiery liquid, instead of to try to kill its bearer.

When the bottle was empty, Levi stepped back. 'I ain't sure one bottle's gonna do it,' he said. 'We want 'im dead, staggerin' drunk, not just feelin' good. Either o' you boys got another bottle?'

John and Will looked at each other silently for a moment. Finally Will shrugged and turned to his horse. He pulled a quart of whiskey from his saddle-bag and carried it around to Levi.

Levi pulled the cork from the untouched liquor and stepped back up behind the bear. The bear rolled his eyes, watching Levi's approach. He abandoned all pretence of anger, opening his mouth for the booze.

'Funny how an animal can develop a taste for that stuff that quick,' John observed.

'Same with a horse,' Tug observed. 'You got to just about pour it down his throat the first time, but after that he'll drink it outa anything he can.'

It took thirty minutes for the bear to drain the second bottle. By the time it was finished, every time he would tip his head up to receive the next drink, he'd fall backwards, so only the ropes around his neck kept him from falling.

Levi stepped back and tossed the empty bottle aside. 'Let's wait a few minutes to let that last drink take effect, then we'll give it a try,' he said.

The others nodded, assenting without

realizing it to Levi's leadership. 'You boys headin' anywhere in particular?' Levi asked.

The three looked at each other in sudden remembrance of reality. 'We, uh, gotta get back to the C bar C,' John said. 'Lige is plumb dead set on stoppin' you a-holdin' that election.'

'It ain't just me,' Levi announced. 'Hiram McDermott is the election judge. He'll be in charge of it. He's lining up some of the other ranchers to help out with it. Travis MacLeash, for one.'

He let the news sink in for several minutes of silence. Tug said, 'Looks like Lige is gonna be standin' all alone, huh?'

'I thought McDermott was just as against women votin' as Lige is,' John said.

'He is,' Levi admitted. 'But he's a law-abidin' man. The law's more important than what he thinks. He don't like it, but he'll put his life on the line to defend it.' He grinned

141

suddenly. 'He even told Deliah he'd let her vote!'

'Naw!' Tug exclaimed. 'Really?'

'Really,' Levi assured him. 'He said he couldn't uphold the law for others if he didn't even let his own wife go by it. Of course he tried to tell her how to vote, then!'

The three laughed together. 'And I bet she told him a thing or two!' Will guessed.

Levi let it go without comment. That got too close to gossip for his comfort level. 'Well, boys, let's see if this works, or if we get ourselves mauled to death by a mad bear,' he said.

The four men moved as one. Each man called to his horse. The four horses relaxed the tension on the ropes and stepped forward. The four jerked their loops from the bear. They whirled and sprinted to their horses, leaping into the saddle. Only then did they begin to retrieve their ropes and coil them.

The bear collapsed on the ground

with the release of the bonds. He lay there for several heartbeats. His head lolled back on the ground. He groaned softly. Then he remembered his wrath. He roared and rolled to his feet. He lunged upright, but he was unable to stop his momentum. He continued on, falling onto the side of his head.

He stayed in that position for several seconds, propped upright by his head leaning against the ground. Then he toppled over onto his side. He roared in anger and confusion and lunged upright again.

He fell backward into a sitting position, and managed to keep from falling on over. He started to growl, but hiccuped noisily instead. The four men roared in laughter.

The bear responded to their laughter by lunging to his feet. He started toward the group, but his feet got tangled together. He tumbled into a heap on the ground.

He lay there, issuing a cross between a growl and a whine for more than a minute. Then he hauled himself to his feet again, only to collapse in the other direction.

'Well, I guess we don't have to worry about him chasing us for a while,' Levi observed. 'You boys ride careful.'

'Uh, much obliged for the hand,' Tug offered.

'Yeah, much obliged,' John agreed

'Me too,' Will said. 'You saved our bacon.'

'Just don't ride up this way for a while,' Levi suggested. 'Our friend there might be a little cross for some time to come. I'd take it kindly if you boys was to think real careful about backin' Lige too far, too. You boys are all right. Don't let him cost you your lives, fightin' for the wrong thing.'

He knew he had asked something they couldn't answer. At least not now. He didn't wait for an answer. He called, 'C'mon, Curly!' and turned his horse back into the timber.

'Hey! That's Ringy's dog, ain't it?' John said.

Tug answered, 'The guy that Lige . . . uh, yeah, sure looks like it.'

'Good dog,' Will said.

'Ringy was a good man,' John said.

'Sure would like to know that story,' Levi said to nobody as the timber closed around him.

11

'Hello the house!'

Levi sat his horse about fifty yards from Victoria Herder's front door.

'Hello the timber'd be smarter'n hollerin' at an empty house.'

Levi whirled toward the voice. Victoria stood at the edge of the trees, shotgun cradled in the crook of her right arm. 'What are you doin' in the timber?' Levi called.

'Stayin' alive.'

'Havin' problems again?'

' 'Bout twice a day's all. They shot out almost every window in my house.'

Levi looked at the house, confirming that most of the windows had been shot out. 'Really tryin' hard to scare you off, huh?'

'They're givin' it their best shot. I been holin' up in the timber, though. I filled one of 'em's fanny with buckshot.

Caught 'im sneakin' up through the timber. I didn't even say nothin'. I was far enough from 'im I didn't figure it'd hurt 'im too bad, so I just cut loose on 'im. He howled like a coyote sittin' in the cactus. He'd run a-ways, then lie down an' roll around, then jump up an' run, then lay down an' roll again. He got back to 'is horse and jumped on, then jumped off and rolled around an' howled some more. Then he got back on and rode off, standin' up in the stirrups an' acussin' a mile a minute. Funniest thing I ever seen in all my born days!'

Levi cackled at her description of the hapless cowboy, almost certainly one of Cambden's lackeys. Then he sobered. 'It ain't really a laughin' matter, though. They'll kill you if you stay here.'

'I thought that was what you was sent up here for. Where you been, while I been fightin' off Cambden's outfit all by myself?'

147

Levi grinned at her. 'Now I thought you were the one that didn't need a nursemaid.'

'Don't you get smart with me! You start throwin' my own words back at me, I'll give you a taste o' this buckshot in the backside.'

'That's why I'm not turnin' my back. I 'spect it's time you came on into town, though. We've got things pretty well set up for the election. Hiram McDermott is going to be the election judge, and he'll round up some of the other ranchers to help.'

'Are you kiddin' me? Hiram Mc-Dermott thinks women shouldn't never even open their mouths till their husbands say they can. How'd you get him to run an election where women get to vote?'

'Hiram's a good man. He doesn't like the idea, but he'll uphold the law. I think we've just about got Cambden isolated as the only one that's going to fight it.'

'Looks like he's done a bit of that

with you, too. Your face'd scare a kid to death.'

Levi nodded.

'They worked me over pretty good. Griff Mulgrew pulled 'em off me. He's the town marshal now, till the election.'

'You don't say!'

Levi started to tell her Griff would be running against her in the election, then thought better of it. Instead, he said, 'Well, are you going to invite me in for supper, or do I have to ask my dog to catch me a rabbit?'

'I saw you found yourself a pair o' ears. Don't want me sneakin' up on you while you're sleepin' no more, huh? Yeah, we'll let your mutt watch for trouble. I could use a square meal. I been afraid to stay in the house long enough to fix much.'

They chatted idly while she fixed supper. They ate pretty much in silence, then leaned back to enjoy a cup of coffee when they had finished. 'I've pretty much decided what my first act as Justice o' the Peace is gonna be. Providin' I get elected, that is,' Victoria announced.

'What's that?'

'Get rid o' the guns in Cambden's Crossin', that's what. I'm gonna pass a law that says everybody has to check their guns in at the marshal's office as soon as they come into town.'

'Won't work,' Levi disagreed.

'Why not? Guns is the biggest problem in town. Everybody's got a gun. Every time anyone gets mad, they try to shoot someone. Get rid o' the guns, and everybody'll work out their differences.'

Levi shook his head. 'That's been tried a place or two. It hasn't worked. It never will. The only people that will get rid of their guns will be the honest people, that respect the law. Then all the good people will be disarmed. Once that happens, anyone with a gun, that didn't turn it in, can do whatever he wants. The only one in town with a gun will be the marshal. Shoot the marshal, and the rest of the town is helpless. And it'll happen. There will always be some that will have guns, or get guns.'

'The fewer guns there are, the less problem it'll be. The town will be safe for women if we get rid of 'em. And with women votin', it won't be hard to pass the laws to do that.'

'But it's the women that need them the most.'

'Why should women need guns?'

'To protect themselves and their families. That's part of allowing women to be something more than helpless victims of whatever the men want to make them do. It's always been pretty much that way, down through history, but it's changing. Women are becoming free to think and act for themselves, and to stand up for themselves. But it's mostly the gun that's made that possible.'

'What do you mean?'

'Well, think about it. As long as there are guns that are small enough and light enough for a woman to handle them, a woman never needs to be afraid of a man. A man never beats up on a woman that has a gun. Men have no way to dominate and terrorize women, if women have guns. As long as she does, she's the equal of a man, even if he is bigger and stronger.'

Victoria snorted. 'Just because she has a gun don't mean she knows how to use it.'

Levi nodded his assent. 'That's true, but if she's smart, every woman in this country will own one and learn to use it.'

'It ain't gonna help her none if she goes up agin' a man with a gun. Men are quicker, an' they can shoot straighter. They been usin' guns a lot longer.'

Levi shook his head. 'It doesn't work that way. Guns are the great equalizer between men and women. In fact, when it comes right down to it, I'd say a woman would have a decided advantage, going up against a man with a gun. There are men who'd shoot a woman, but they'd hesitate first. To a man, they'd hesitate. Even I would, I 'spect. And that instant of hesitation gives the woman a pretty big advantage.'

Victoria sipped her coffee while she thought about it. 'Aw, it ain't never gonna come to nothin' anyway. I'm just kiddin' myself. Even if I was to get elected, it wouldn't last. They'll take away the right to vote again, an' then what'll women have? They'll be right back where we was afore.'

Levi shook his head. 'It'll never happen. The only way women can lose the right to vote now, is if they, themselves, give it up. It would take their vote to change it now. No woman in her right mind is going to vote for a law that takes away her right to vote, any more than she would for a law that would take away her right to own and use a gun.'

Victoria snorted again. 'I still think it's a good idea to get rid of guns.'

'Like I said, it's been tried. Towns have tried passing laws forbidding guns within the town. All it ever accomplished was to make the honest people helpless victims of the ones that didn't follow the law. I've had to go into three different towns just to get the people armed again, so they could control the lawless elements.'

'I thought that was what the law was for. That's why a town has a marshal.'

Levi shook his head again. 'The best the law can ever do is try to make crime dangerous for the criminal. The law can react after a crime has been committed. The law can't keep laws from being broken. It can't keep people from being robbed or killed or raped. After that's happened, the law can try to catch whoever did it. But the law will never run out of law breakers to chase after, and they can only chase them after the crime's already been done. The law can't protect anyone. The only one that can protect you is you. That's why you been lyin' out in the trees. You know I can track down anyone that shoots you, and shoot him, or hang him. But I can't protect you, even if I stayed here all the time.'

'You'd be more protection here than runnin' around the country.'

'Not a lot more. The only one that can protect you is you. And you can't protect yourself against a man with a gun, unless you've got a gun yourself. That's especially true of a woman, 'cause she ain't as big or as strong as a man.'

'But if he's faster an' better with his gun, I still can't keep him from killin' me. Or whatever.'

'True, if it comes to a real shootout, and if he manages to hit you first. But as long as you have a gun, and he knows you have a gun, he's not going to be nearly as apt to try anything. It's too dangerous. Why do you think Cambden's boys haven't just walked up to your front door and shot you?'

'Cause I'd cut 'em in two with this Greener!'

'Exactly. The thing that makes you the safest that you can be is that you have a gun, and you know how to use it. You can't take that away from people. If you try, you'll be worse than Cambden, trying to make everyone powerless except you.'

'You shoulda been one o' them politicians! It ain't possible to argue with you.'

They were interrupted by Curly's low growl. 'Company comin',' Levi said softly. 'You'd best get on the floor.'

Victoria was already moving. She sprawled out on the floor facing the front door. Her shotgun was in her hand.

Levi slipped silently through the front door. He hugged the wall of the house, moving quickly around the corner away from the direction the dog was watching. Curly continued to growl softly.

'C'mon, Curly,' Levi whispered.

Not waiting to be sure the dog responded, he moved quickly, crouching across the yard and into the trees. Once in the foliage he straightened. He moved noiselessly from tree to tree, gliding like a silent shadow. No stick snapped beneath his foot. No leaf rustled.

Well away from the house, he whistled softly. 'Blue. Come here, boy.'

A few minutes later his horse appeared, walking with his head down, seeking the sound of his master's summons. Levi quickly dug into his saddle-bags. Bringing out a pair of moccasins, he exchanged his boots for them. He tucked the boots into the saddle-bags, and he moved away from the horse.

The time Levi had spent with the Shoshone Indians was not wasted. He had learned to fight, to brave pain stoically, and the craft of woodsmanship nearly as well as any member of the tribe. At tracking he could better the best of them. In the use of a gun none within that tribe could even approach his speed and skill.

Now he looked and acted more like a Shoshone Indian than a cowboy. Curly followed in his footsteps, matching his new master's movements and silence.

He circled the house, moving to the top of a ridge that overlooked the yard. Staying just across the crest of the ridge, he slid along, watching and listening intently.

Fifteen minutes after he had slipped out of the house, he caught his first glimpse of his quarry. Thirty yards in front of him a man stood beside a tree. He had a rifle, with its barrel steadied against the tree trunk. He was watching Victoria's house over the top of the gun barrel.

From this vantage point, the front door of the house was clearly in view. Levi realized with a start that it was only the dog's early warning that had allowed him to leave by that door before the man was in place. A tide of gratitude and appreciation for his new-found companion welled up within him.

He stepped into the clear. His hand hung loosely right at his gun butt. He said, 'Odd way to call on the lady.'

At the sound of his voice, the man exploded into action. He whipped the rifle around, squeezing the trigger as he turned. Even as he did so, he dived away from his position, sailing over the top of a downed tree trunk.

The bullet from the rifle thunked harmlessly into a tree trunk four feet from Levi. He snapped a shot from his pistol after the man, but it passed over him as he dropped behind the log. Levi ducked behind a tree, even as bark flew from a spot just beside his head.

He cursed himself silently. He had expected the man harassing Victoria to be one of Cambden's cowboys. Instead it was immediately evident he was a gunman, and good at his job. His movements were lightning quick, well rehearsed, and very, very dangerous. Only his own training and long experience had kept him from being the victim instead of the hunter.

Levi looked at his dog, crouched against the ground beside him. 'Get his horse, Curly. Take his horse.'

As though he understood, the dog slunk away through the timber. Levi shrugged, at a complete loss whether the dog understood the command. He moved away from the tree he had taken refuge behind, careful to keep it between him and his adversary.

When he was a few feet from the tree, he began to move on a circular course again, moving to flank the gunman. His silent form floated eerily through the timber, as though never quite touching the ground. He might have been a wisp of smoke, impossible to hear and visible only in occasional tiny glimpses.

Ten minutes later he crept up toward the log behind which the gunman had taken refuge. He was not there.

Backing quickly into deeper cover, Levi looked around. Nothing moved. He crept to where he could see the yard in front of Victoria's house. Just as he looked, his dog came into view. Held securely in his teeth was one rein of the gunman's horse. The horse obediently plodded behind.

Levi was not the only one to notice. He heard a soft curse less than thirty feet to his right, through the brush. Moving swiftly on cat feet, he followed the sound of the voice. The gunman stood, frozen in disbelief, watching his horse led away by a dog.

'Drop the gun!' Levi ordered.

The gunman whirled toward his voice, firing as he turned. The angry whine of a bullet passed Levi's ear, even as his own gun barked its answer. His bullet smashed through the gunman's neck, sending a shower of blood and flesh into the leaves of a plum bush behind him. He dropped like a steer in a slaughter house, without sound or feeling.

Levi lowered his gun without even ensuring the man was dead. He automatically thumbed out the spent cartridges and replaced them from the loops at his belt. He called down the hill, 'It's all right, Victoria. I got him.'

Less than half a minute later Victoria stepped into the door of her house. She called back up the hill, 'One o' Cambden's hands?'

'Gunman,' he called back. 'Never saw him before.'

He sighed. Well, he'd have to lead the man's horse back up here, then hoist the body onto it and tie it across the saddle. Then he could turn it loose and it would go home to Cambden's place, if it were one of his horses. If it was the gunman's horse, no telling where it would consider home. Either way, it would take him someplace. One place was just as good as another. The gunman certainly no longer cared. By the time he reached wherever the horse would take him, Levi and Victoria would be in Cambden's Crossing. Any more assassins Cambden sent here against her would find only an empty house.

12

'Things are shapin' up pretty good, but Cambden's fit to be tied.'

Levi glanced the length of the main street of Cambden's Crossing. The street bustled with activity. Buggies and wagons were tied up in rows the full length of the street. Saddled horses filled every hitch rail. Looking down the street he could see a virtual tent city set up outside town, where people had come in to camp until after the election. It had become an occasion to celebrate.

'Sure looks like the whole country's gettin' excited about it,' Levi agreed. 'It's hard to believe there's this many people that live around here. And the election's still two days away.'

'The ballots came in earlier today,' Hiram said.

'Good. Did you check 'em over?'

Hiram nodded. 'I opened 'em up and looked at 'em. They seemed to be right. All the names o' people that are runnin' are on there. There's a blank line under each one too, to write in somebody's name if their name ain't on the ballot.'

'No sign of Cambden yet though, huh?'

'Nope. I seen a couple o' his men in town every day, lookin' things over. They keep tellin' me how mad he is, but they ain't sayin' nothin' about what he's cookin' up.'

'Do they know the ballots have come in?'

Hiram nodded again. 'That Texan was here when they come in. He got his horse an' rode out less'n an hour afterwards.'

Levi pursed his lips. 'Well, that might give us an idea. You don't suppose Cambden had some different ballots printed somewhere, do you?'

Hiram frowned. 'What? Where? Whatd'ya mean?'

Levi shrugged. 'I'm not sure. I'm just tryin' to figure out what I'd do, if I was him. He's gotta know he can't stop the election. There's too much excitement about it. If he tried, he'd have the whole country after him. He's gotta know he can't tell people who to vote for and who not to. He's bound and determined women aren't gonna vote, and no woman's gonna get elected. So the first thing he'd have to do is be sure the ballots don't have any women runnin' for office on 'em. The second thing he'd have to do is be sure him or his men are runnin' the election, so they can turn women away that try to vote.'

'There ain't no way he can do that!' Hiram protested. 'If he tried, he'd start a war.'

Levi nodded. 'So instead o' that, he'll have to have two ballot boxes, and his people where the votin' is bein' done. That way, the women's ballots can be put in one box, and the men's in another. After the election, then, he

166

can just get rid of all the ballots in the women's box.'

Hiram sputtered in anger for half a minute before words would come out. 'Why he'd never . . . Why . . . Well, how's he gonna do that? I'm the election judge. And Fred Miller, from the Rockin' M, and Bart Langstrom, from the Cross L, and Travis MacLeash, from the Wagon Wheel are all helpin'. Cambden or any o' his boys ain't even gonna be involved!'

Levi frowned thoughtfully. 'I know. That's why I'm worried. We know Cambden's going to try something. The only way I can figure for him to get control of things now, since he couldn't scare Victoria into withdrawing, is what I just said. I just can't think of any other way.'

'So how do you think he's gonna try it?'

'I don't know. The only way I can think of, is if he rides into town with his whole outfit, puts Slim back in as town marshal, then has him declare your group ineligible to run the election. Then Slim could appoint his own group, that would be Cambden and some of his men.'

Hiram blanched. 'He's probably got twenty-five men behind him. Would he try that, do you think? There ain't any o' the rest of us has more'n half a dozen hands. He could sure outgun us, if he did that. Aw, he wouldn't try that, would he?'

'Well, you know Lige better'n I do. Would he?'

Hiram thought about it for a long moment. 'He would. When Lige gets somethin' in his teeth, he just don't never let loose of it. And he's got the guns. Besides his reg'lar hands, he's got that Texan workin' for 'im. He's just a gunman, is all he is. And he's got Nevada Carlson. He's another one. And Lee Henson, he's another. Nate Wilson you shot the other day here in town, but he's still got at least three or four others that are outright gunmen ridin' for 'im. The rest o' his outfit ain't no slouches with a gun neither. Me an' my boys can handle a gun fair enough, but we ain't no match for the likes o' Cambden's outfit.'

Levi nodded. 'Well, then it makes sense. That's probably what he'll try. And he won't want to do it quick enough to let us telegraph for the army. That means he'll probably try it on Monday. That's tomorrow. That gives us the rest of today to get ready.'

'How you gonna get ready for that?'

Before Levi could answer, they were interrupted by a sudden burst of noise down the street. They walked hurriedly toward a growing crowd a block away.

Elbowing their way through the crowd, Levi and Hiram stopped abruptly. Victoria Herder stood spraddle-legged in the middle of the street. Facing her was the C bar C gunman who called himself Nevada Carlson. The gunman was grinning. 'So you're the old hen that thinks she can be a marshal, huh? You don't look like no marshal to me. You look more like my grandma.'

A ripple of chuckles and giggles barely broke the sudden silence of the crowd. Victoria's face suffused to bright red. 'Why you bandy-legged little pipsqueak,' she spluttered, 'if you were my grandson I'd turn you over my knee and spank your backside.'

'And what if I decide not to let you do that, Grandma?' the gunman taunted. 'Or better yet, suppose I'm some drunk cowboy over at Paddie's, and you gotta come and haul me off to jail. How you gonna do that, Grandma? You gonna shake a willow switch at me and tell me to march myself off to jail?'

The taunt was rewarded with the ripple of laughter, slightly louder than before. Levi Hill frowned, but did not interfere.

The red of Victoria's face deepened perceptibly. 'I'll shake this willow switch,' she said, brandishing the double barreled shotgun. 'And if you don't shut your flappin' jaw and get on about your business, I'll give you a dose of it right now.'

The gunman grinned broadly but his eyes remained cold orbs of expressionless fire. 'Would you now, Grandma? I'm sayin' you wouldn't. I'm sayin' you couldn't use that thing on a man if you was close enough to more than sting him with it.'

'You just try me and see, you big-mouthed bag o' hot air!'

The gunman's expression did not change. 'All right. I'll just do that. Here. I'll tell you what I'm going to do. I know I'm way too fast for you to deal with if I draw against you. I'd kill you right where you stand before you could even swing that scattergun of yours around. So here's what I'll do.'

As he spoke, he slowly drew his gun, using his thumb and one finger. 'I'm going to lay my gun right here on the ground, on this nice hard spot here, where it won't get all dirty.'

As he said it, he did as he was saying, laying the gun down with the butt toward himself. 'Now I'm gonna back away a couple steps.'

He did so. 'Now here's what I'm gonna do, Grandma. I'm going to walk forward, bend over, pick up my gun, and then I'm going to even the score with you. You see, I'm the guy that was out there in the timber the other day, that you thought it'd be a great big joke to fill his backside with buckshot. You did. I was far enough away it scattered real good. Even so, I had six pieces o' your buckshot dug outa me. Now it's judgment day, Grandma. I just happen to have six pieces o' lead in my gun. And when I pick up my gun, I'm gonna give back those six pieces o' lead you gave me. Only you ain't gonna be alive when the sixth one hits you. And you ain't gonna do nothin' about it, Grandma. You're gonna stand there and watch me, and cuss a blue streak, and die. Because you ain't got guts enough to look a man in the face and shoot him with that man's shotgun you're so fond of carryin'.'

As he spoke, the red slowly left

Victoria's face. It was replaced by an ashen grey. Even her lips disappeared in the solid greyish white pall that spread across her visage. People scattered from behind Victoria and from behind the gunman. The crowd at both sides began to edge backward, giving room for the two.

'The time is now, Grandma,' the gunman said. The grin was gone from his face. He stepped forward one step. He stepped the second step. He bent forward. Victoria swept the shotgun around, pointed directly at the gunman. He gripped the butt of his gun.

'Don't pick it up,' Victoria said. Her voice had more pleading than threat.

'Shoot me then, Grandma,' the gunman said. ' 'Cause I'm gonna shoot you if you don't.'

'Don't do it,' she pleaded.

He picked up the gun. His thumb swept almost negligently across the hammer, cocking it. It lifted toward Victoria's chest.

'Drop it!'

The gunman's eyes darted sideways. Griff Mulgrew stood three steps behind Victoria and a couple steps to one side. He had a thirty-thirty carbine to his shoulder. The hammer was cocked. The barrel stared squarely at the gunman's chest. 'Drop the gun!' the marshal ordered. 'There ain't gonna be no shootin' here!'

The gunman looked momentarily uncertain. 'This ain't your business, Marshal,' he said. 'This here's between me and the lady.'

'Not no more it ain't,' Mulgrew argued. 'It's bein' a matter o' my business, now that it's in town. Now drop the gun.'

Nevada Carlson mentally calculated his chances. 'I don't think so, Marshal. I think I can kill you and the lady both, before you can squeeze that trigger.'

'But you forgot to count me.'

Levi's quiet voice dropped a complete hush on the street. The gunman's eyes darted toward him. Levi stood with his gun drawn, facing the gunman. 'Now do like the marshal said. Put that gun away, and get out of town.'

Nevada's eyes darted back and forth from the marshal to Levi, to Victoria and back to Levi. Slowly he lowered the hammer of his Colt and dropped it back into the holster. Griff lowered the hammer on his carbine, then lowered the rifle. Victoria staggered a step sideways, as though suddenly bereft of strength. Levi also holstered his weapon.

'You shouldn't have horned in, Hill,' the gunman said.

The excited babble that had erupted in the crowd stopped as if someone had switched it off. All eyes were drawn to Nevada, then to Levi, then back to Nevada.

'I don't like people buttin' into my business,' the gunman said. 'You been a problem here one time too many. I'm callin' you, Hill. Go for your gun.'

People again scattered from the presumed line of fire, crowding into each other, knocking several people down in their haste to get out of harm's way.

'You don't need to do that,' Levi said. His voice was calm and even. 'You know you couldn't get out of town, even if you could beat me. Just let it go.'

'I'll let it go when you're dead,' Nevada gritted.

As he spoke his hand streaked upward, holding his gun. It happened so swiftly that nobody even saw Levi draw. One second he was standing as though totally relaxed. The next second his gun was in his hand, jumping and spitting death at the startled gunman.

The gunman stopped with his gun still pointing at the ground. His face twisted in a grotesque grimace. He rose to his toes, leaning forward, then collapsed onto the ground.

Excited babble again erupted in the crowd. People began to crowd around Levi and Victoria, talking rapidly. Griff walked over to the dead gunman. He turned him over with his foot, then bent to retrieve the man's gun. He lowered the still-cocked hammer and tucked the gun into his own waistband. Then he once again lowered the hammer of his carbine.

Victoria looked as if she were about to be sick. Levi put an arm around her shoulders. 'C'mon over to the café and sit down a while,' he said.

She allowed herself to be led across the street to the Chuck Wagon Café. When she was seated with a hot cup of coffee in front of both her and Levi, she finally spoke. 'He's right, Levi. I couldn't.'

'I told you it was a whole lot harder'n you thought. It ain't an easy thing to look a man in the eye and kill him.'

'I didn't never think it'd be like that. I thought it'd be just like shootin' a rattlesnake. That's what he was. He wasn't nothin' but a poisonous rattlesnake, an' I knew that, but I couldn't shoot 'im. I couldn't even shoot 'im to save my own life!'

Levi said nothing. He let her sip

her coffee until the trembling of her hands had steadied. She was the one who broke the silence. 'I can't run for marshal. The whole town'll know I couldn't shoot nobody if I had to. They'll think I ain't fit to be the marshal. They'll be right.'

Again Levi said nothing.

She continued. 'I gotta take my name off the ballot.'

Levi finally spoke. 'There is no reason you couldn't be Justice of the Peace. That doesn't call for you to use a gun, or to try to overpower drunk cowboys. That calls for common sense and some knowledge of the law.'

She sighed heavily. 'I'll think about that.'

'You better think pretty fast,' Levi said. 'The election's day after tomorrow.'

And a whole lot of trouble comin' one day quicker'n that, he told himself silently.

13

'Sure, have you been seein' the sign?'

Levi searched Griff's face for an indication of his elation. 'What sign?'

'Victoria Herder has just been puttin' up a sign on the front wall o' the feed store, where the election will be.'

'Really? What does it say?'

Griff stuck a pose, positioning one hand as though following the words of the sign. As he spoke, he moved his hand along, following the location of the words. 'I am asking everyone that votes to vote for me, Victoria Herder, for Justice of the Peace. I am asking everyone to write in the name of Griff Mulgrew for town marshal. I am not running for marshal. Signed, Victoria Herder, Candidate for Justice of the Peace.'

'You don't say! Well, that just might give you the votes you need. Maybe you and Connie will have a job to get married on yet.'

'Are you knowin' what else 'twould mean, if the election is goin' that way?'

'Uh, no, what?'

'That's meanin' that we'd be havin' a Justice of the Peace right here.'

'Well, yeah. If the town elects a Justice of the Peace, then the town will have a Justice of the Peace. That seems reasonable.'

Griff squirmed with impatience. 'That's not what I'm meanin'! Of course 'twould mean the town would be havin' a Justice of the Peace if the town votes for a Justice of the Peace! But what I'm tryin' to be sayin' is that, sure and a Justice of the Peace can do weddin's as well.'

'Ah, that's the excitement. But there's already a preacher in town. Preachers marry people.'

'Not me an' my Connie, I'm thinkin'. She's not likin' the idea of askin' a preacher to marry us, and maybe havin' to listen to a sermon on her sinful ways, and maybe even bein' told he wouldn't be doin' it.'

Levi shook his head. 'I don't think that would likely happen. Anyway, if Victoria gets elected, I'm sure she'd be plumb tickled to make that her first official duty.'

'Sure, where is it you're goin' now? I'm seein' a lot of the men goin' over to Walt's.'

'I've called a meeting of the businessmen. I was just coming over to ask you to come too. We need to plan a strategy to deal with Cambden when he shows up.'

'Sure, and you're thinkin' he'll show up, then?'

'Count on it.'

Griff accompanied Levi across the street. The room fell silent as they walked in. Without preamble, Levi said, 'I've asked you all here to plan a strategy to deal with Cambden. I think we can be confident he'll show up sometime tomorrow.'

A large man with a gold watch chain stretched across his ample stomach spoke up. 'There is no reasonable supposition that we can stand against Cambden and his entire brigade of well disciplined fighting men.'

Levi smiled. He looked around at the gathering of the businessmen of the town. Roughly fifteen men crowded the front part of Walt's Saddlery. 'The odds really aren't that bad,' he responded.

Isaiah McCall, owner of the mercantile store, who had spoken before, disagreed. 'There is no reasonable supposition that we can stand against them,' he repeated. 'Cambden has carefully chosen his hands for their competence with firearms and their willingness to employ them nefariously. We are an honest and hard-working lot, whose experience with such things is minimal.'

'That's beside the point,' Levi said. 'I'm not asking any of you to stand out in the street and draw against any of Cambden's men. That would be foolish. What I'm saying is this. We have the authentic, official ballots. If he wants to subvert this election . . . '

'Would you two stop usin' all them four-bit words?' Hank Tillman, owner of the livery barn protested. 'The rest of us ain't got no idea what you two are talkin' about when you do that.'

'I'm sorry,' Levi apologized hastily. 'What I'm saying is this. If Cambden wants to stop the election, or control it, he has to do two things. He has to get ahold of the ballots. I'm guessin' he's had other ballots printed, with no women's names on them.'

'The only woman on the real ballots is Victoria Herder,' somebody protested.

Levi nodded. 'But that's one woman too many for Cambden. So we're guessing he'll try to get rid of the ballots, and replace them with his own. Then, the other thing he'll be trying to do, is to stop any women from voting.'

'That shouldn't have been allowed in the first place,' the same voice offered.

Levi ignored the interruption. 'To do that, he'll have to get rid of the real election judges, headed by Hiram McDermott here, and put his own men in their place. Now think about it from his position. That's not going to be easy, with the town as full of people as it is.'

'And gettin' fuller all the time,' Hank agreed. 'They's a tent-town on all sides that's bigger'n the town itself.'

'All we need is a circus to have a grand celebration of epic proportions,' Isaiah concurred.

Levi tried to regain the focus of the discussion. 'The point is this. The only hope he has of doing what he wants to is to come in with as big a show of force as he can muster. If he can bring in a large party of men, say thirty or forty, well armed, and showing they're ready for a small war, he'll assume the whole town will roll over and play dead.'

'What choice would we have?' that pesky voice asked.

'Stand up to him,' Levi said. 'Let him know that if he wants to take over the town, he's going to have the fight of his life. If we do it right, we can show him that when he's in the worst possible position. He'll almost certainly come in right down the main street, in a big show of force. If we wait until his whole outfit is in the center of town, then show him that he's in the middle of two rows of townspeople, armed with shotguns, he won't dare touch a gun.'

'Why shotguns?'

'Because shotguns at that range are a whole lot worse to face than a pistol, or even a rifle. They cover such a wide swath that even a bad shot can't miss with 'em. And they don't carry so far. By the time a shotgun blast gets clear across the street, it's not likely to kill anyone. So even the shots that are missed won't be a big danger to the townspeople on the other side of the street.'

'You mean it would mitigate the

casualties incurred by friendly fire amongst our own troops,' Isaiah offered.

Levi grinned in spite of himself. 'Spoken like a field general.'

'Or a politician,' that voice in the back suggested. 'Why don't you talk like a real person, Ike?'

Isaiah's face flushed, but he remained silent. Hank asked, 'Where you gonna get all these people a-linin' up on both sides o' the street?'

'Right here, for a start,' Levi replied. 'This is your town, not Cambden's. Fight for it.'

'But Cambden owns my store.'

'Mine too. I just rent it from him.'

'I don't even rent mine. He just takes a percent o' what I make for settin' me up. I don't see how I kin buck 'im thataway.'

Levi nodded. 'I know that most of you are beholden to Cambden in one way or another. But that doesn't give him the right to run your lives. It sure doesn't give him the right to make his own laws, or to refuse to obey the laws of Wyoming Territory. If you let him do this, then the army will come in, and you'll have nothing at all. The only chance you have to take control of your own town and your own lives is to stand up to the man.'

'Well, he's got a couple less professional gunmen than he started out with.'

'Three less. I killed one at Victoria Herder's the other day.'

'Mulgrew's wearin' the marshal's badge. He's a good start in any fight.'

'And he'll be right out there in the street with me,' Levi assured whoever spoke the words from the back of the room.

'As will I,' Isaiah volunteered.

A moment of silence erupted into a dozen small conversations. After it had run on for several minutes, Levi held up his hands for silence. As the noise subsided, he said, 'Now I know we can enlist quite a few from the ranchers, homesteaders and ranch hands that are already in town. The fact that they're here pretty well indicates they're not planning to listen to Cambden. But I need to know for sure how many of you I can depend on. I want everyone that's willing to stand and fight against Cambden to come over to this side of the room.'

Nobody moved for quite a while. Then Isaiah and Hank stepped over beside Levi. They were followed by two others, then by most of the rest of the men present. Only four men stayed on the other side of the room. Levi addressed them. 'You fellows are free to go, then. Nobody's going to try to make you do what you can't see your way clear to do.'

The four looked at each other sheepishly for a moment. One of the men moved across the room to join the others. The other three left. Before conversations had a chance to start, Levi said, 'How many of you own a shotgun?'

Most of them raised their hands.

'OK. How many of you own a rifle?'

Again, most of them raised their hands. 'How many don't own either one?'

Three men raised their hands. Levi said, 'Isaiah, do you have three extra shotguns you can lend these three men?'

'Most assuredly I do,' Isaiah responded.

'OK, then, here's the plan,' Levi said. 'Right after sun-up tomorrow morning we'll put a man on the roof of the church with a telescope. It's on the end of town that Cambden will most likely come from. Just to be safe, I'll put a man a mile out of town the other direction, just in case Lige gets foxy and decides to circle around and come in the other way. When either man sees his outfit coming, he'll give the word. Then we'll ring the church bell. When you hear the church bell, grab your gun and get into place where I tell you. We'll also spread the word around town so everybody that's already here will know, when the church bell rings, to get off the street. We don't want a bunch of women and kids where they're likely to get hurt.'

'What if Cambden gets the word?'

'We'll have to take that chance. I'm a lot more worried about someone getting hurt than I am about him learning of our plans. Now, I want six men that are good with a rifle.'

'I thought you was gonna just use scatterguns.'

'We are, on the street. But I want six men with rifles on the roofs, three on each side of the street. If they have to shoot, they'll be shooting down, toward the ground. There won't be much chance of their hitting somebody on the other side of the street.'

'What do you mean, 'if they have to shoot'?'

'Well, to tell the truth, I don't expect anyone to have to fire a shot. When Cambden sees that he's boxed in on both sides, and the whole town is standing up to him, he'll back off. He's not going to get himself and his men all killed when he knows he can't win.'

'You don't know Cambden. When he gets his dander up, he don't back down from nothin'.'

'Maybe not, but his men will. They're not crazy. They're loyal to him, but they won't deliberately die for him. When they all see how the wind blows, Cambden will most likely be standing in the street all by himself.'

'Except for his gunhands.'

Levi shook his head. 'They'll be the first to ride out. They live by their guns, and a gunman that can't weigh the odds doesn't live long. Their only loyalty to Cambden is the wages he pays. When they see the situation, they'll be the first to turn and ride out.'

'I'll believe that when I see it,' Hank argued. 'I think we're settin' up the worst bloodbath the territory's ever seen. They're gonna stand an' fight to a man, and we're gonna be just tryin' to see who's still standin' when

191

the smoke clears. It's gonna be just like Shiloh, all over again. There ain't half of us gonna make it through this alive, you mark my words.'

'If I thought it would come to that, I wouldn't even ask you to do it,' Levi said. His voice was soft, but it almost quivered with intensity. 'I've never in my life asked a man to do something I thought would get him killed. And if it does come to shooting, I'll be the first target they shoot at. I'll be right in the middle of the street, right in front of Cambden. I give you my word.'

He looked around the room, making eye contact with every man present. Nobody offered anything more. 'OK,' he said. 'Let's move out and see how many other men you can enlist. Those that don't have guns, or don't have ammunition, see Isaiah. Isaiah, you keep a tab, and the territorial government will pay for it.'

Isaiah shook his head. 'I will neither expect nor accept remuneration from the territorial governor or from South

Pass City. It is the privilege of the citizenry to provide the means for the defence of their own liberties.'

'As you wish,' Levi said. 'I just want you to know the territory will stand good for it if you want paid. Let's go.'

There was a general rush from the room. Levi watched them all go, hoping against hope he wasn't sending them to their deaths.

14

Pounding hoofbeats stirred dust from the road into Cambden's Crossing. Butch Hennessey leaned over his saddle horn, hugging the horse's neck. His hat-brim in front was blown up against the crown of the hat by the wind of his horse's speed.

At sight of his approach, people at that end of Main Street began scurrying toward the sidewalks, clearing the road. Butch raced through town, then hauled back on the reins, bringing his horse to a sliding stop in front of the church, just at the far edge of town. He leaped from the saddle, sprinting for the church door.

He jerked his hat from his head as he lunged through the door. An instant later, the church's bell began ringing frantically.

At the far end of Main Street, Levi's

head jerked up. He and Griff Mulgrew had been engaged in conversation. It was chopped off in mid-word, as both swung their attention to the clanging bell.

'That's it,' Griff said. His voice betrayed excitement tinged with fear. 'That's the signal. Must be Butch ringin' it.'

'Get your men in place!' Levi agreed. 'We can't have more'n fifteen minutes, tops.'

Both men began running. Griff began to yell at people in the street. 'That there's the signal! Get off the street! Get your women and kids outa the way! All you men, get where you're supposed to be.'

The street instantly resembled an ant hill some child had begun to stir with a stick. People began running in all directions. Women grabbed their children and hurried down the sidewalks. One woman, holding two small children in her arms, tripped on her dress and fell in the middle of the street. Two men immediately went to her aid. One picked up the children, while the other helped the woman to her feet. Neither stopped to ask if she were hurt. They silently hurried her from the street, into the door of a millinery shop. As she entered, the lady who owned the shop grabbed her arm, hustling her and her children to the back of the store where other customers had gathered. She urged them to sit on the floor.

As though some great wind were blowing the pieces of humanity aside, the street cleared. In less than five minutes, an eerie hush descended. Men with rifles peered over the false fronts of stores, then ducked back out of sight. The town changed, in those scant minutes, from the picture of a frontier town at the peak of holiday activity to the picture of a ghost town. Levi's skin crawled as the old familiar warning of impending battle passed across the back of his neck.

From the door of the gunsmith's shop he watched. A child's cry, quickly hushed, sounded out of place from some store. A man's curse, low and hushed, floated from the livery barn. Signs that were hung in front of businesses swung back and forth in the breeze, squeaking softly. A door slammed somewhere far away.

'There they come,' someone at the far end of the street called.

'They're comin'.' 'Here they come.' 'There they are,' other voices repeated softly to those around them.

The announcement rippled along the length of the street. The unnatural silence returned.

Stepping to the sidewalk, Levi could see the heads of several horsemen bobbing rhythmically over the top of the rise at the edge of town. As he watched, the rest of the men came into view.

He recognized Lige Cambden riding in the lead. The big chestnut stallion he usually rode trotted with high, prancing steps. His huge neck bowed gracefully. Lige told everyone who'd listen that he rode that horse because it reminded him of a horse a king would ride.

Behind him the Texan and Lee Henson rode, slightly to either side. Behind them the rest of the C bar C crew rode, four abreast. Levi couldn't be sure, but he thought that in the first rank of the regular crew were the three men who had whipped him in the bar. They were the same ones he had kept from getting killed by the grizzly they had decided to rope and brand.

There must have been thirty men in the group. They rode tall and straight. Every face reflected a deep seriousness, but no fear.

At the edge of town, Lige held up his hand. The band of men stopped, as if controlled by a single will. Lige scanned the empty street, scowling. Others in the group began to glance around. Nobody spoke.

Levi stepped into the street. He walked to the center of the street and stopped, facing Lige and his outfit, at least three hundred yards from them.

He was positioned directly in front of the gunsmith's shop, nearly three-fourths of the way through town. If Lige approached to within fifty feet of him, the entire group would be between the two rows of businesses.

Lige studied him in silence for a full minute. Then Griff Mulgrew stepped out from the other side of the street, taking his place beside Levi. The midmorning sun cast a pair of long shadows in front of them.

Victoria Herder stepped out of a store and walked into the street.

'Victoria, this ain't no place for you,' Levi said softly.

'I'm guessin' it is,' she retorted. 'This here brouhaha is all on accounta me in the first place. It's only right I stand with you to deal with it.'

'Sure and you're already knowin' you can't be shootin' a man with that scattergun o' yours,' Griff said.

Victoria's face reddened, but her chin jutted forward stubbornly. 'I been thinkin' on that,' she said. 'I ain't gonna back down from usin' it twice. 'Specially if I get a chance to use it on Lige Cambden. You can count on me. I'll come through.'

Further conversation was cut off by Lige lifting his reins and nudging his horse into action. His men followed wordlessly. He rode silently, walking his horse, until he was less than thirty feet in front of the trio in the street. He reined to a stop and stared at them. Levi returned the stare calmly. 'Mornin', Lige,' he said. 'Come into town so your boys can all have a chance to vote tomorrow?'

Lige opened his mouth twice, closing it silently each time. The third try, words came. 'Get outa my town, Hill. And take that foul-mouthed woman an' that dumb Irishman with you. This thing's gone as far as it's gonna go. I got different ballots printed up. I told Slim he's the marshal again, until the election tomorrow makes it official. And I got some of my boys that'll be takin' care of the votin' place, so there ain't gonna be no women's votes counted in this country. Not tomorrow, an' not never.'

'Is that a fact?' Levi said. 'Now just who elected you king?'

Lige's face reddened, but he did not react. Instead he said, 'This is my town, Hill. It's gonna stay my town.'

Levi shook his head. 'No, Lige, it isn't. It never really was, even though you pretended it was. This is a free country. Just because you own the biggest spread around here, that doesn't make you any different from the old drunk that cleans the livery barn. You're just one man, just like he is. And the fact is, he has just as much say about how this town and this country is run as you do: one vote.'

Lige's jaw clamped. Muscles bulged at the hinge of his jaw. His face paled. Levi's hand brushed the butt of his gun as he watched the change. 'Get outa the way, Hill,' Lige said softly. 'I ain't wantin' to kill you, but I sure can. If you don't get outa my way right now,

I'll shoot all three of you down, right here in the street, and we'll ride right across your bodies. There ain't no way you can stop me.'

'You're wrong about that,' Levi said. He raised his voice, so it would carry to every man riding for Cambden. 'The whole town's against you, Lige. You and your men are hemmed in on both sides. If anyone starts shooting, there won't be a man alive in the middle of this street in three minutes.'

He gave his words an instant to soak in, then called out, 'Isaiah. Bring your men out.'

Isaiah stepped out of the front door of his store. He waved a hand toward the church. Immediately the church bell rang several times.

As the tones of the bell died away, men stepped out of the stores, the full length of Main Street. Each man carried a double barreled shotgun. All were pointed at the riders, totally exposed and grouped together in the middle of the street. A ripple of surprise and fear passed the length of the group.

One of Cambden's riders glanced up, then stiffened. 'They're on the roof too, Lige,' he called.

As one, the eyes of Cambden's crew lifted and scanned the roofs of the businesses. The men with rifles stationed there showed themselves.

'What kinda nonsense is this?' Lige blustered.

Levi ignored the question. 'Lige, this is a civilized country. You can't jam your will down other people's throats. Not any longer. There's going to be an election here tomorrow. Women will vote. At least one woman will be on the ballot. You can either accept it, and change with the times, or you can leave and go somewhere else and start over, or you can try to fight a losing battle and die right here in the street. It's your choice. But there's no sense in dying for something you can't change anyway.'

Lige glared at Levi. He looked first

one way then another, mentally tallying up the guns against him. Levi could feel his resolve growing to fight to the death rather than back down.

The Texan obviously felt the same resolve growing, and wanted no part of it. His soft drawl broke in on the rancher's thought processes. 'If you're plannin' on openin' up a fish shoot in this here street, count me out,' he said. 'I ain't lived this long fightin' bad odds an' worse situations. I reckon as how I'll just be ridin' out.'

The gunman turned to Hill. 'Hill, I've heard of you. I was sorta hopin' to have a chance to face you, just you'n me. I ain't sure that woulda been a good idea neither. Maybe I'll see you around sometime.'

Levi nodded wordlessly. The Texan wheeled his horse and trotted past the assembled crew.

As he left, the man at Lige's right spoke up. 'That goes fer me too, I reckon,' Lee Henson said. 'I can't remember never walkin' out on a man in a fight, but they's always a first time. Anyhow, I don't reckon they's no fight started yet, has they? So I'm pullin' out afore they is. Lige, I know this ain't no very fair way to do you, so you kin just keep whatever I got comin'.'

He lifted his reins and turned his horse, trotting after the departing gunman. Half a dozen emotions crossed Lige's face. John Dally rode up beside his boss. 'Lige me'n Tug 'n Will are sorta thinkin' the same. We whupped up on Hill, here, on accounta you told us to. He coulda pulled his gun an' kilt us, but he didn't. He took a whippin' instead. Then the other day he had a chance to get even with us, without even raisin' a hand. He put his own life on the line for the three of us instead. We're sorta thinkin' maybe we're backin' the wrong man here. We decided Hill's a better man than you'll ever be, an' we ain't about to back you against him. We'll be pullin' out too.'

The three men reined their horses to

the side of the street and followed the gunmen out of town. As they passed the ranks of Cambden's hands, others began to break off and follow them wordlessly. Lige watched helplessly as every hand but one rode away, leaving him alone facing Levi, Griff and Victoria. The only man left to back his play was Slim Collins, the man who had been Lige's hand-picked marshal before Levi came. Levi felt a swell of admiration for the man who was willing to die with his old boss rather than desert him.

Levi spoke. 'Give it up, Lige. It's all over. Come into town tomorrow and vote. It will be the beginning of a new time. It'll be just as good a time for you as it is for everybody else, if you'll let it.'

Cambden glared helplessly. His mouth opened and closed like a fish left to gasp on the bank. Finally he whipped his horse around and rode away. The trio stood watching him.

Suddenly Lige stopped. He turned

his horse sideways in the street, right at the edge of town. He whipped his rifle from its scabbard, levelled it, and squeezed the trigger. A puff of smoke wafted away from the end of the barrel. Victoria grunted and fell sideways into the street.

Lige shoved the rifle back into the scabbard. He wheeled his horse, jamming the spurs into the stallion's sides. The horse leaped forward, reaching full stride in four jumps. Lige leaned low over the saddle horn, jabbing the horse continually with his spurs.

There was an instant of stunned surprise. Then half a dozen shotguns fired impotently in the general direction of the fleeing rancher. Three of the rifles on the roof barked, but none came close. The three shots were followed by a sudden fusillade, but the streaking stallion never faltered in his stride.

Levi whirled to Victoria. 'How bad are you hit?' he asked.

'I ain't sure,' she gritted 'Got me here in the side.'

She moved her hand from her left hip. It was covered with the blood that had already soaked through the coarse fabric of her pants. 'Get the doc,' Levi ordered Griff.

'Sure, he's already a-comin'',' Griff said, pointing.

Levi followed his finger and saw the doctor running their way. 'Then you tend to Victoria,' he said. 'I'll go after Lige.'

'Sure an' I'll be goin' with you,' Griff said.

Levi shook his head. 'It's my job. You stay here and make sure the election goes the way it's supposed to tomorrow, in case I'm not back by then. That's your job.'

His jaw was set and his eyes smoldered as he walked toward the livery barn.

15

'C'mon, Curly!'

Levi cursed himself for not having his horse saddled. He had to waste the time running to the livery barn, saddling up, then working his way through the press of people jamming the main street of Cambden's Crossing. If his horse had been saddled, he could have been after Cambden in seconds. Now the man was already out of sight.

He trotted Blue, saving his strength for a long chase. He had been involved in far too many of these situations to think he could run his quarry to ground quickly.

'Gotta catch up with him before tomorrow,' he told his horse. 'Otherwise, he just might be mad enough to circle around somewhere and try to stop the election yet.'

Half a mile out of town he suddenly noticed Curly was not following as he always did. Instead, he was out in front, nose and tail in the air. He loped along in an easy, ground-eating stride, following the faint trail the rancher had left when fleeing.

'You don't suppose he's followin' the trail o' that stud horse o' Cambden's, do you, Blue?'

Levi's horse gave no indication he heard. Levi only frowned, and nudged the horse to keep pace with the big shaggy dog.

The trail cut across a patch of bare red earth. A fresh set of horse tracks cut straight across it. Levi reined in and studied them swiftly. 'That's Cambden's stud all right,' he affirmed.

He looked at the dog again. The dog was loping in a straight line, right beside the visible trail of their prey. 'Well what d'ya know?' Levi marveled. 'That dog's even got a nose. He figured out who we were following, and just started following his trail for us.'

He nudged his horse into motion. 'Well, let's keep up with 'im, Blue.'

As if he understood, the big gelding swung into an easy lope, keeping pace with the dog. Levi held him back, allowing the dog to stay about two hundred yards ahead. 'First time I've ever followed a man without having to worry about him cutting back,' he said. 'If Lige does try to set up an ambush, the dog'll let us know before we're in range. We can just concentrate on tryin' to catch up with him.'

An hour later the fleeing rancher's tracks changed. 'Looked back from the top of that hill and didn't see anyone chasing him, so he dropped back to a good trot,' Levi said. A grudging appreciation tinged his voice. 'At least he's still got his senses enough to take care of his horse.'

When Curly slowed to a trot, Levi tugged gently on the reins to tell Blue to do so as well. 'Dog's startin' to get tired,' he observed.

They crossed a small stream. Levi stopped, keeping his distance behind Curly, while the dog stopped and drank. Then, when the dog moved ahead, he and the horse both slaked their thirst before moving on.

Three hours later Curly stopped abruptly. His nose raised a notch higher. His tail went down between his legs. 'Trouble,' Levi breathed.

He swung Blue into a stand of timber and circled the clearing the dog stood in. When he was almost abreast of the animal, he called softly. 'C'mon, Curly. Let's circle this way.'

The dog glanced toward him, then back at the trail they had been following. Levi frowned, looking around. They had climbed nearly two thousand feet in elevation, and were at least fifteen miles from Cambden's Crossing. They were within a mile or two of the spot Cambden's hands had roped the grizzly, several days before.

The thought brought a grin to Levi's face. 'That still tickles me,' he confided in his horse. 'Darndest thing I ever saw.'

The grin faded as he studied the area. Curly lowered his head, then began to crouch lower and lower. 'Somethin's sure botherin' that dog,' Levi breathed. 'What d'ya bet Lige's holed up at the far side o' the clearin', just waitin' for us to show ourselves.'

He moved back into the trees and circled farther around the clearing. From the corner of his eye he saw his dog abandon the trail. Still crouching, he began to slink toward the tree line in a path to intersect Levi.

Levi steered Blue carefully around deadfalls and loose rocks that would make enough noise to give away their position. He felt, more than saw, Curly take up his more normal position about two steps behind them. He scanned the timber ahead of them intently.

He silently drew his thirty-thirty carbine from his saddle scabbard. As quietly as possible, he levered a shell into the chamber. He rested it on the pommel of his saddle, with his finger inside the trigger guard.

They were nearly around the clearing when the dog let out a low growl. Levi pulled the reins, stopping his horse. He could see nothing. He nudged Blue gently. The horse hesitated an uncharacteristic moment before responding, then began to move forward slowly, silently.

The dog growled again. Levi frowned, but did not stop. The timber thinned, opening into another clearing, less than a hundred yards across.

He jerked the reins, stopping his horse. Curly growled again. Two-thirds of the way across the clearing, Elijah Cambden sat his horse. The horse was sideways to them. Lige was turned in the saddle, so he faced them squarely. He watched them over the barrel of his thirty-thirty carbine.

'Stop it right there, Hill,' he called.

Levi cursed himself silently for not listening to his dog. 'There's no sense in runnin', Lige,' Levi called back.

'There's no place left to run to. A man that shoots a woman can't run far enough in this country. You'd just as well come on back and face the music.'

As he talked, Levi swung his own horse side-ways, allowing him the option of using his own rifle if forced, or if the opportunity presented itself. From the corner of his eye he saw Curly slink away. With his belly against the ground, the dog began a circuitous path around the clearing. 'He's going to try to get up behind Lige!' Levi marvelled silently.

'I ain't goin' back there with you or nobody else,' Lige responded. 'The town can curl up an' die for all I care. I started that town. I pumped the life blood into it, when it woulda died without me. I staked most of those guys. An' that's the thanks I get. Just as soon as some new-fangled idea comes along, the whole town turns against me. Well they can all go jump in the crick, now. I'll start a different town, an' every rancher in the country will come there for what they need, and the Crossin' will just dry up an' blow away. That's what'll happen, mark my words.'

Levi shook his head. 'You pretty well lost the chance to do that when you shot Victoria,' he said. 'Now you got to face that.'

'There ain't no way I'm goin' back there to face that,' he said. 'They'd just hang me right off the bat, the way they're all turned against me now. She deserved to die, though. She surely did.'

'Nobody deserves to die for following the law, Lige. Anyway, she won't die.'

'She won't? I didn't kill 'er?'

'Nope. You was a little low an' wide. Looked to me like the bullet might've bounced off her hip bone, maybe. Tore quite a hunk out of her, an' she's losin' some blood, but I'd guess she'll live all right.'

'Well, now, ain't that just the thing!' Lige exclaimed. 'Now they'll have that danged election tomorrow, an' likely put her in as Justice o' the Peace, an' you wanta arrest me an' take me into town there an' be tried by her? Now wouldn't that just be somethin'! No sir, that there ain't a-gonna happen, Hill. You best just drop that gun now, or I'll have to shoot you off that horse.'

Levi had lost sight of his dog. From time to time he had noticed his location by grass moving slightly, and knew the dog had almost succeeded in circling the rancher. He had no idea what command to give the animal to tell him to attack.

One try's as good as another, he decided.

Aloud he called, 'Get 'im, Curly!'

The dog stood up from the tall grass less than ten feet straight behind the rancher. He ran silently and gave a great leap. Just as he struck the rancher he snarled wickedly.

'What the . . . ' the rancher yelled. His horse shied violently. The unexpected movement of the horse, the sudden fright, and the weight of the hurtling animal toppled the rancher from the saddle. His carbine fired harmlessly into the air as it struck the ground.

The rancher rolled to his feet. He whipped out his pistol. He jerked first one way, then the other, trying to find the dog. Curly was nowhere to be seen.

'Drop the pistol,' Levi called. 'I don't want to have to shoot you.'

The rancher whirled, glaring at Levi. Instead of complying, he jammed the pistol back into its holster and lunged for his horse. Leaping into the saddle he whirled toward the line of trees.

His horse ran three steps, then stopped abruptly. Lige almost lost his seat at the unexpected and sudden stop. He jammed his spurs into the horse's sides. The horse squealed in pain and fear. His ears were pinned back tight against his head. His nostrils flared. His eyes rolled

Belatedly, Lige looked to his right. Lumbering from the trees, a huge grizzly bore down on the rancher and his mount. From his position, Levi could clearly see the fresh marks of a C bar C burned into the side of the bear.

Lige's horse began to buck frantically. Lige cursed and grabbed for the saddle horn. His right foot lost the stirrup. The horse sunfished out from under him, leaving him flailing in mid air. He tried desperately to cling to the reins, but the panicked horse jerked them from his grip and fled, squealing in terror.

The bear was on the rancher in an instant. Whipping out his pistol the rancher emptied it into the enraged beast. It had no apparent effect whatever. The bear knocked Lige down and began to maul him with fangs and claws.

Levi sank his spurs into Blue's sides. 'Get over there, Blue!' he yelled. The horse shuddered in fear, but still responded obediently. He lunged forward, ears flat, head low to the ground. From nowhere, Curly emerged from the grass, impelling himself into the side of the angry bear, tearing a piece from its ear and twisting away.

With an enraged shriek the bear whirled away from Lige and swiped at Curly with a front claw. The dog was already out of reach, circling for another attack.

When he was twenty yards away, Levi turned his horse sideways, levering his rifle on the bear. Lige struggled to his hands and knees and started to crawl away. The bear wheeled and swiped a huge front paw at him. It caught him in the ribs with a sickening whack, picking him up and rolling him onto the ground.

Levi's rifle barked. A puff of smoke wafted from the end of the barrel. The bear grunted, then turned toward him.

The puff of smoke had scarcely left the end of the barrel when Levi had jacked another cartridge into the chamber and fired again. Again the bear grunted, but continued to approach.

Cambden groaned and struggled to his hands and knees again. The bear whirled with incredible speed and lunged at him, sinking his fangs into the rancher's neck. He heaved himself up to his hind legs, standing nearly eight feet tall. The rancher hung limply, his neck securely gripped in the jaws of the giant grizzly.

Levi pumped round after round into the animal's heart, firing as fast as he could work the lever of his carbine, until the hammer dropped on an empty chamber.

He reached into a saddle-bag, fumbling desperately for the ammunition he knew was there. Curly crouched beside him, growling fiercely. The hair on his neck and back bristled upright, but he did not move.

After what seemed an eternity, Levi's fingers closed over a handful of shells. He jerked them out and began thumbing them into the magazine of the rifle. The whole time the bear stood stock still. Lige dangled motionless from the bear's jaws. The animal made no sound.

When he had five shells into the gun, Levi levered one into the chamber and raised the rifle again. He did not fire. The bear did not move. The dog crouched as though made of stone. The only motion was the trembling and twitching of Levi's horse, too frightened to hold still, too obedient to move.

They stayed that way for fully half a minute. Then the bear started to move. Almost imperceptibly at first, he began to lean backward. Then he began to pick up speed, collapsing backward like a giant tree felled by a woodsman's axe. He hit the ground with a crash. Red dust welled up around him. He lay perfectly still.

Released from the bear's grip, the rancher rolled off the animal. He too lay without moving.

Levi watched for any sign of movement. There was none. He nudged his horse. A shudder passed through the big gelding's hide. He took a step forward, then another. Still nothing else moved.

Ever so slowly the horse moved toward the prone grizzly. His hide quivered constantly. Beside him, the square-jawed dog walked, stiff-legged, tail between his legs, nose stretched forward.

Levi kept the gun to his shoulder. The supine bear stayed in his sights. When he was ten feet from it, he stopped his horse. He lowered the rifle. He stepped from the saddle. He walked over to the bear. No breath came from its nostrils. It was dead.

Levi heaved a great sigh. He knelt beside the rancher, knowing before he did so that the man was dead. When he had confirmed it he rose. He spoke to his horse and dog. 'Well, fellas, I guess that takes care of that.'

Curly came to him then. Whimpering softly he nuzzled Levi's hand. Levi took the side of the dog's head in his hand, scratching him affectionately. 'You are some dog, ol' boy,' he said. 'You are some dog.'

His horse shoved him with a wet nose. 'All right, Blue, you don't need to go gettin' jealous,' Levi scolded. 'You're one fine horse, too. I'll find you some oats when we get back to town.'

He looked around the clearing. 'Well, I guess we'd best find Lige's horse, then we can haul him back to town. We just might get there in time to see the first woman elected in Wyoming Territory.'

THE END

We do hope that you have enjoyed reading this large print book.

Did you know that all of our titles are available for purchase?

We publish a wide range of high quality large print books including:
Romances, Mysteries, Classics
General Fiction
Non Fiction and Westerns

Special interest titles available in large print are:
The Little Oxford Dictionary
Music Book, Song Book
Hymn Book, Service Book

Also available from us courtesy of Oxford University Press:
Young Readers' Dictionary
(large print edition)
Young Readers' Thesaurus
(large print edition)

For further information or a free brochure, please contact us at:
Ulverscroft Large Print Books Ltd.,
The Green, Bradgate Road, Anstey,
Leicester, LE7 7FU, England.
Tel: (00 44) **0116 236 4325**
Fax: (00 44) **0116 234 0205**

Other titles in the
Linford Western Library:

THE SAN PEDRO RING

Elliot Conway

US Marshal Luther Killeen is working undercover as a Texan pistolero in Tucson to find proof that the San Pedro Ring, an Arizona trading and freighting business concern, is supplying arms to the bronco Apache in the territory. But the fat is truly in the fire when his real identity is discovered. Clelland Singer, the ruthless boss of the Ring, hires a professional killer, part-Sioux Louis Merlain, to hunt down Luther. Now it is a case of kill or be killed.